"Where's Fin?"

"He's in the front room, doing his summer project for school."

"He's doing *what*?"

Matteo flicked Porsha a look to find her staring at him and grinned. "I know, wonders never cease, right?"

She shook her head and fisted her hands on her hips, her blouse pulling taut across her front—not that he was noticing or reacting in any way, shape or form. *Neighbor. Friend. Fin's parental figure!*

The mental mantra was getting tired. Stepping in as Fin's manny for the summer had been an easy offering, one that Porsha had eventually accepted and one that was going swimmingly in all ways but one—*this*.

The incessant pull he felt toward her, the attraction, the chemistry...

Experience told him it should have eased by now.

Instead it was doing the opposite.

Maybe that was denial for you—evil.

But seeking out a fling right on one's doorstep was never a good idea. Especially when he had no interest in commitment. Short-term, long-term, any kind of term.

And then there was Fin to consider, a boy who'd already been through enough upheaval to last a lifetime.

No, denial was the only option.

Dear Reader,

Just as you can't choose your family, you can't choose your neighbors, either, and like many of us, we've not always been so blessed. We have some tales, let me tell you. But our neighbors now are the most wonderful, generous and caring of people. Lucky us!

But the very idea that the love of your life could so happen to be the person over the fence, across the hall, in the next room was an idea I instantly fell in love with—so much so it became the central theme for my next three books!

For this one, Matteo and Porsha live in London's highly fashionable Notting Hill. Despite being neighbors, they've never met until now... As their lives take a very different but no less pivotal twist, they are thrown together, or rather brought together, by an AWOL piece of lingerie(!) and a gorgeous, if a little mischievous, seven-year-old boy who, like our hero and heroine, deserves a happy-ever-after.

This one is all about love and family, taking what life throws at us and coming out stronger for it. Happy. Content. Together.

I hope you love it as much as I do!

Rachael xx

UNEXPECTED FAMILY FOR THE REBEL TYCOON

RACHAEL STEWART

ROMANCE

Harlequin® ROMANCE

ISBN-13: 978-1-335-21601-4

Recycling programs for this product may not exist in your area.

Unexpected Family for the Rebel Tycoon

Harlequin Enterprises ULC
22 Adelaide St. West, 41st Floor
Toronto, Ontario M5H 4E3, Canada
www.Harlequin.com

Printed in U.S.A.

Rachael Stewart adores conjuring up stories, from heartwarmingly romantic to wildly erotic. She's been writing since she could put pen to paper—as the stacks of scrawled-on pages in her loft will attest to. A Welsh lass at heart, she now lives in Yorkshire, with her very own hero and three awesome kids—and if she's not tapping out a story, she's wrapped up in one or enjoying the great outdoors. Reach her on Facebook, Twitter (@rach_b52) or at rachaelstewartauthor.com.

Visit the Author Profile page at Harlequin.com.

For the best neighbors in the world,

Peter, Pippa and Abi.

Thank you for being the BEST!

xxx

Praise for
Rachael Stewart

CHAPTER ONE

MATTEO WAS TAKING a rare moment to soak up the equally rare rays of the British sun when he found himself wearing a baby-pink bra like a pair of silk earmuffs…

Si, that's right, a bra.

A very pink, very delicate, very much *not* his bra.

Pulling it from his head, he straightened in his lounger and fixed his hair, all the while frowning up at the fence over which it had appeared. There was a rustle and a scuttle, possibly a snigger, but it seemed the owner was making no attempt to accompany said underwear. He heaved a sigh of relief—*Grazie a Dio!*

He'd had his fill of women throwing their delicates at him over the years. But never had it happened in his own property. Quite literally, on his own turf.

Not that he'd spent much time here since purchasing the Notting Hill home a few years ago. But now that he'd hung up his football boots, injury seeing him permanently benched and retired at the ripe old age of thirty-two, he intended to change that. Hence the lounger, the iced water and the attempted session of—dare he say it—*mindfulness*.

That was until…

He stared at the intricate mix of lace and satin. Freshly washed, judging by the scent, and still damp in parts. As though its airing had been cut short when it embarked on its short flight.

The sound of voices—muffled, distant and gradually elevating—forced him to stand and take a closer look. Through the lattice top to the fence, he couldn't see anyone in his neighbour's garden, but the sliding doors to the rear of the house were ajar, the noise emanating out.

He scratched the back of his head, eyed the rest of the laundry still safely secure on his neighbour's washing line. For a forced introduction, this was right up there with the weirdest, most forward…

But what should he do?

Toss it back and pretend to be none the wiser?

Or walk around and hand it back?

He really wasn't the type to fall for such an obvious ploy, but…

He'd never met his neighbour before. She'd moved in while he'd been in Europe touring the many property developments he had underway. But he'd seen her coming and going. A petite brunette, no nonsense demeanour, always in black or a variation thereof and classy by all accounts…she didn't strike him as the type to resort to such lengths.

Then again, he'd never have pegged her as the type to wear pink under all that monochrome either.

The voices continued, ever more harried…

He could hardly ignore the ruckus, and he certainly couldn't ignore the bra.

Looking at his designer sun lounger—owned for years, never before used—he bade it farewell. His therapist wouldn't approve, but who was he to ignore a woman in need?

He was his own worst enemy. His therapist knew it, he knew it, but then he should've introduced himself long before now.

And the lounger really wasn't him. Not the lounger or the prescribed mindfulness.

Bra in hand, he strode through his house and out the front door. Hopping over the wall that divided his six-storey townhouse from hers, the dramatic charcoal-black facade to his standing bold against the pastel blue of hers, he went to ring the bell, but the front door was already opening.

He backed up as a woman hurried out. Not his neighbour. No, this one was also short but stout and, oddly, soaking wet. She barged past him, cheeks and eyes blazing as she donned her jacket, flicking out her sleek black ponytail and muttering under her breath.

'Ms Smith, please!'

Now, there was his neighbour, desperation in every strained feature as she yanked the front door wide and hurried after her, bypassing him entirely and hollering over the garden gate as she gripped it, 'We have a contract!'

'Not any more we don't.' Ms Smith waved a hand over her head without halting. 'You're on your own, Ms Lang. I'd wish you luck, but I fear it will be wasted.'

Matteo's neighbour stared after her and he gave her a moment, two, three…

Now what?

Was this what it felt like to be normal, ordinary, *invisible*?

Matteo took a tentative step forward. 'Hi…?'

She spun to face him, surprise rolling with the desperation.

'Can I…?' Her voice trailed off as her eyes drifted to his hand, to the item dangling carelessly from it… 'Is that…?' She waved a weak finger at it, her eyes launching back to his face. 'Did you…?'

'Oh, *Madonna mia*, no!' Palms outstretched, incriminating pink fabric swinging, he launched himself forward and hurried to explain. 'I was in the garden minding my own business when *this*—' he thrust it in the air '—came over the fence.'

A catcall sounded down the street, the item drawing attention, and he crumpled it to his chest. 'It had nothing to do with me…' And judging by her horrified expression it had nothing to do with her either. '*Honestly.* Nothing at—'

'Bombs away!'

The war cry came from behind him, and she straightened, her eyes widening as she looked past him at her open door. 'Finlay Lang, don't you—'

He turned with her and found himself face to airborne missile a nanosecond before it exploded against his head in a shower of water. Stunned and soaked, he spluttered, 'Whoa!'

'Oh my God. Oh my God. I'm so sorry.' She rushed forward, panicked hands fluttering all over him, uncaring where they touched as she sought to dry him off. 'What a day. What an absolute mare of a day.'

He swept his sodden hair off his face. Okay, so it wasn't the introduction he'd expected, but if she kept patting him up and down like that, he'd have more than just a soaking to worry about.

'I think a towel might do a better job, don't you?'

She stilled. Lashes lifting until her eyes met his. This close he could see they were hazel with an alluring ring of honey and as he watched, they dilated. Slashes of pink appeared in her olive-toned cheeks, her lips parting as she registered the position of her hands. One resting over a twitching pec, the other just below his belt and too close for comfort.

She jerked back, hands fisted. 'This can't be happening.'

She said it more to herself, her gaze zoning out as though willing it to be so.

'I think my damp clothes might suggest otherwise.'

He gave her his most charming smile, eager to show no harm was done, and she backed up another step as a towel miraculously appeared to her right.

'Sorry, Aunt Porsha,' came a whisper.

She grabbed the towel and thrust it at him. 'You'll have to forgive my nephew, he's a little… he's…well he's…'

'I'm a little hooligan.'

She winced as the young lad stepped out from behind her, brown hair as floppy as Matteo's own when it wasn't tamed—much like now.

She touched a hand to the boy's shoulder. 'Ms Smith never should have called you that.'

The lad shrugged. 'I don't care, she was—bloody hell!'

'Fin!'

Blue eyes blinked up at him, mouth to the floor. 'You're—you're…'

'Enough, Fin.'

'But, Aunt Porsha!' The boy pressed his lips together, eyes bugging out as he looked up at his aunt. 'But he's…'

Matteo's smile was automatic, born of two decades in the limelight as he patted himself down with the towel. 'Yes, I am.'

Confused hazel eyes lifted to his. 'Yes, you are, *who*?'

'I'm—'

'He's Lucky Luca, Aunt Porsha!'

'Lucky who?' Her brow furrowed deeper and Matteo gave up on the towelling off to give her his whole attention.

'Matteo De Luca.' He went to hold out his hand, belatedly remembering the bra still in it and, after adding it to the towel in his other, tried again. 'I'm your next-door neighbour.' He gestured to his house. 'I live just there…'

Fin stepped between them and grabbed Matteo's hand. Shook it with more ferocity than his slight frame would have suggested possible. 'I'm Finlay Lang. And this is my aunt. Aunt Porsha. She's my new mum. Kinda… I've not seen you here before. Why haven't I seen you before? Have you seen him before, Aunt Porsha?'

Matteo chuckled over the detailed introduction and interrogation. One that, judging by his aunt's pinched expression, she was none too pleased about.

'Well, it's a pleasure to meet you, Fin.' He returned his handshake. 'Can I call you Fin?'

'Yeah!' The boy gave a gappy grin. 'Can I call you Lucky?'

'You can call me whatever you like.'

'Just wait until my friends hear about this! I'm going to get my phone. Can I get a picture? I can get a picture, right?'

'Sure.' Matteo looked at Porsha. 'If that's okay with your aunt?'

Too impatient to wait for his baffled aunt to respond, Fin raced off.

'Are you some TikTok star or…?' She smoothed a hand over her hair, hugged her middle as she eyed him. Increasingly edgy now the boy had gone. 'I'm sorry, I'm really not up to speed on the world kids live in.'

'No apology necessary. I'm a footballer. *Was* a footballer.' Why did that still have to stick in his throat so much? 'Recently retired.'

'Ah!' Her brows lifted. 'That explains it.'

'It does?'

'Football is about the only thing capable of holding his attention for longer than five minutes.' She gave a weak smile that had him wishing he could earn the real thing.

'Not you so much though.'

A hint of pink crept back into her cheeks. 'I didn't say I didn't care for the sport…' She nipped her lip, drawing his eye to the alluring fullness of her mouth. Soft and glossy. ' More that I haven't got the time for it.'

'Maybe you could make the time,' he said forcing his eyes back to hers, 'and I'll take you and Fin to a match one day?'

She gave a tiny huff—gratitude, surprise, disbelief?

Hell, he couldn't blame her. He couldn't believe

he'd asked. Was he that caught up in the lad's excitement that he was losing his head? Was he that bored of life as he now knew it that he was seeking excitement with the neighbour he'd only just met? Or was he just perturbed that she seemed to have no awareness or interest in him whatsoever?

But then, neighbours hung out, right? It was a normal thing to do…

'I'll—I'll think about it.' Her gaze drifted to the street and she ducked her head. 'Would you like to come inside? I think we're…'

She gestured behind him with a subtle hand and sure enough, they had a mini audience gathering. Notting Hill and its influx of famous faces saved him from such attention usually, but standing on a woman's doorstep dripping wet, clutching pink undies hardly flew under anyone's radar. Famous or not.

'Grazie.'

She backed up and he hurried inside, his trainers squeaking against the plastic sheeting that covered the beige carpet of her entrance hall.

'Please excuse the mess.'

'Mess?' It was an orderly haven of clean lines and neutral colours. Everything seeming to have a place and positioned just so…save for the very thin trail of devastation right through the middle that consisted of puddles and tiny strips of rubber—unfilled ammo in the shape of water bombs. 'This isn't a mess.'

'We're mid-renovation, but I'm starting to think the plastic sheeting might be worth keeping…' She hurried to pick up the pieces of Fin's trail as she led them through to the back. 'Fin! What are you doing? I'm sure Mr Luca needs to be getting back and—'

'There's no rush,' he assured her. 'I don't have any plans…'

Aside from your healthy dose of mindfulness that you're clearly trying to avoid!

But could he help it if such a novel distraction had landed in his lap…or rather on his head?

Porsha bit her cheek, eager to keep her cool.

He was hot.

Like, seriously hot.

The kind of hot you expected a filter to produce, not the naked eye.

And she was gawping behind the lens when she was supposed to be taking a photo.

But then, he was still clutching her bra. Her very pink, very private bra.

It wasn't often Porsha was lost for words and action, but in the last two years, Fin had brought her to a stunned standstill too many times to count. And this scenario truly took the biscuit.

'Can I…? May I…?' She waved a loose finger and he jumped forward, muttering something in Italian. Colour rushed his cheeks—*all* the boyish charm—and her heart skipped a beat as he thrust it at her.

Their fingers connected, his heat enough to scorch her skin…her bra too!

She snatched it back with a gulp. 'Thank you.'

'Like I said, it just appeared out of the blue.'

'It just…*appeared*?'

They stared at one another. How was it possible her underwear could soar over the garden fence… take flight by its own volition?

There was a stifled giggle. Then another. Fin was trembling head to foot, eyes burning into the tiles of the kitchen floor.

'*Fin?*'

His head shot up. 'I'm sorry, Aunt Porsha, it was an accident. I saw this cartoon, and they had the bombs and the—the *thing* and some sticks, and together they managed to make them go really far and I—well, they made it look easy. And you and Miss Ellen were talking really loudly, and I wanted to get out of your way so you could work and …well, I didn't think it would fly too.'

'You were shooting water bombs with my *underwear*?'

'Trying to, yeah.'

Porsha's cheeks had to be as pink as the bra in her hand, words failing her.

'Well, you have to admire the lad's ingenuity.'

'Ingenuity?' she choked out. 'Copying something he saw in a cartoon?'

Fin pouted. 'I did ask if you would help make a real catapult.'

'And I told you I would at the weekend.'

'That was two weeks ago.'

'I've been busy.'

'You're always busy.'

'I would be less busy if we could keep a nanny for longer than a week so I can get some work done, Fin.'

A throat cleared to her left—one very attractive, very masculine throat—and Porsha gave herself a mental slap. What was she even doing? Arguing with a seven-year-old like he could possibly understand where she was coming from...and in company too.

'About that photo?' Matteo said. 'We could take it outside. I'm sure you must have a football—we can get some action shots in.'

'For *real*?' Fin bounced on his feet.

Matteo looked to her, again seeking permission, and she nodded. The sooner this was done, the sooner she could get Mr Sexy Footballer out of her home and get back to work.

And how do you propose working when you have no nanny?

She blew out a breath, ignored the look Matteo sent her way and followed a racing Fin outside. While he fetched his ball, Porsha focused on re-pegging her bra, grateful to have her back to her unexpected guest as her cheeks burned deeper.

Why had she chosen *today* of all days to wash her delicates—a whole line's worth?!

'Got it!' Fin declared, making her jump as Matteo gasped.

She turned to find the man rubbing his head, the ball rebounding through the air.

'Fin!' Porsha admonished.

'Sorry, Lucky!'

'My bad,' the man said, evading her eye as he went after it. 'I wasn't paying attention.'

Wasn't paying attention or wasn't paying attention to Fin because his focus had been on her undies enjoying a good airing! For the love of…

She swallowed and threw her focus into the task at hand—playing photographer to her budding footballer. 'Come on then, let's see some action for the camera.'

She stood back and let Matteo take over. The man was a natural, getting Fin to do as he asked, lining up the best shots…and Fin listened. Listened and did. Following instruction after instruction. No backchat. No rolling of the eyes. No complaining. Just doing as he was told. By a grown up.

And Porsha was so captivated by the novelty that she lost track of time, forgetting all about work and the board meeting she was supposed to be hosting over Zoom. She even got as far as relaxing and enjoying the moment with them.

'Did you see that, Aunt Porsha? Did you see it?'

She laughed. 'I saw.'

'I nailed it!'

'You did.'

'Did you get it on camera?'

'Of course, I did.' She turned to Matteo. 'You're a good teacher.'

'Helps to have a good pupil.'

They shared an easy smile, the awkwardness from before slipping away as swiftly as Ms Smith had exited.

'You think I'm good?' Fin snagged Matteo's attention once more.

'Well, don't you?'

Fin's chest puffed up. 'It helps when you're getting taught by the best.'

And was Matteo the best? Porsha had no idea.

'Not sure I'd agree to being the best any more, but I'll take it.' He ruffled Fin's hair, the affectionate gesture warming Porsha's heart as she snapped another pic.

Maybe this impromptu meeting wasn't so bad after all…not if it had Fin happy and contained for a spell.

'Why don't you both—' She broke off as her own phone started to buzz in the back pocket of her jeans, reality returning with a grimace-inducing thud. It would no doubt be her assistant wondering why she wasn't online yet. She hurried over to Fin and gave him back his phone.

'Why don't you check over the photos while

I take this call?' She pulled her phone out and looked up at Matteo. 'Is that okay with you? I just need a minute.'

'Of course, take your time. I'm having as much fun as he is.'

He grinned and her stomach swooped. Definitely far too sexy. And far too kind.

'Thanks!'

She hurried inside before her traitorous body could make her any more uncomfortable and took up position by the window so she could keep one eye out. Though she trusted Matteo to be good and kind and everything he appeared to be, as Fin's guardian she wasn't comfortable letting them out of her sight.

'Hi, George,' she said as soon as her assistant answered.

'Hey, where are you? I've been holding everyone off, but Charles is getting tetchy. His flight to New York takes off soon and he wants this crisis addressed before he's airborne.'

'I know, I know. I'm sorry. I've been held up. I've lost another nanny and—'

'*Another*? But that's—'

'Fifteen in as many months, I know.'

Outside Matteo was creating makeshift goalposts with some upended plant pots she still hadn't got round to filling, Fin his eager assistant, and she smiled.

'Do you need me to postpone the meeting?'

'What—*no*. Absolutely not.' Porsha raked her fingers through her hair. She couldn't keep bailing on work because of Fin. Not at her level. You didn't get to be CFO of a *FTSE 100* company ducking meetings because your childcare had bailed.

'Porsha?'

'No—I…' She looked back out the window. At the child she couldn't connect with and the man who had no such issue. Could she ask him? Would he mind? Did she have any other choice?

'Look, I can just be honest with him,' George was saying, 'I'm sure—'

'Don't you dare, George. Charles would never understand. You know that.'

'But, Porsha, last time you did a call with Finlay, you ended up with a feral cat trying to scratch your eyes out.'

She had, but then…

'He's over his rescuing waifs and strays phase now.'

'And the fire starter phase? Because I'm not sure anyone's ready for another nerve-provoking demo of fire containment.'

'Every drawer is childproofed now, and I got rid of the candles.'

'Still, if there's trouble, he'll—'

'Find it, I know.'

And they were wasting precious time reliving it all when her job was on the line. 'Can you buy me five minutes, George? Tell them I'm having technical issues.'

'Wi-Fi down and you're hooking up to mobile data? Sure thing, boss.'

She hung up, her gaze returning to the window and the scene that was so perfect it could be a sign of domestic bliss…a father and his boy spending quality time together. Something Fin would never get to experience.

Porsha swallowed the pang of it, rolled her shoulders back and stepped outside.

'Watch, Aunt Porsha! Watch!'

She gave a strained smile. She'd love to watch. Only she couldn't. She had five minutes, and the clock was ticking.

Matteo looked up, gave her a brief smile before positioning himself between the goalposts and giving what she was sure was a feigned attempt at a save, letting the ball in at the last minute.

Fin raced around the garden, arms in the air. 'Goooaaalll!'

Porsha clapped. 'Bravo, Fin!'

Matteo straightened as she walked up to him. 'Everything okay?'

Her heart skittered. When was the last time someone had stopped to ask her that?

'Yes…no…not really.' She struggled between the lie and the truth, the concern in his warm brown eyes making her dizzy.

'Let me guess, you used to be indecisive, but now you're not so sure?'

'What?' And then she laughed, his tease registering and fracturing through the tension. 'Would you believe I used to be the decisive one in the family?'

A family that had shrunk with the sudden loss of her sister two years ago…

'Sorry.' He raised a hand. 'Bad joke.'

'Not at all, more a bad day.'

'So you said. I think your words were "an absolute mare." Does it have something to do with the scary lady doing a runner when I arrived?'

'You mean the nanny?'

'Is that what she was…?'

'*Was* being the operative word. She quit.'

The summer stretched long and impossible ahead of her. School was out. Holiday club had kicked Fin out. Her parents were travelling Europe. And she…she was rapidly failing her late sister's child.

'And I take it you're supposed to be working?'

'Yes.' She breathed through the pain, the frustration…she couldn't fail. Not at this. 'I have a meeting I need to chair in five minutes and—'

Fin came running up to them. 'Can we go again, Lucky?'

Matteo dragged his gaze from hers to smile down at Fin. 'Defo. Just give me a moment with your aunt.'

Fin fist-pumped the air with a whoop and raced off. 'Best day ever!'

'At least he's happy,' she said, watching him go.

'He is. And if you're happy leaving him with me, I'll watch him for you. You go and take care of your meeting.'

'It's like you've read my mind, I was going to ask, but…' She sighed, her eyes returning to Matteo. 'It doesn't seem fair when we've only just met and I'm sure you have some place else to be.'

'I'm retired, remember?'

She gave a scrunched up smile. 'You really don't mind?'

'I really don't. Now, off you go. Consider me your…what do they call it? Bro-pair? Manny?'

She laughed, her shoulders lighter than they'd felt in days. 'Matteo the Manny…' she shook her head in wonder '…it has quite the ring to it.'

'Lucky Luca, Manny Matteo.' He shrugged. 'It seems my name befits alliteration.'

Fin burst through the middle of them. '*Manny*— yuck! I'm sticking with Lucky.'

'You do that, kid,' Matteo called after him, chuckling. 'Now go, Porsha. Take your call. Fin and I will be just fine…as will your underwear.'

He gave her a wink and chased after Fin. Thank heaven. Because the last thing she needed was him witnessing her full-on blush. What was it about this man that had her all hot and flustered?

You mean, aside from the fact he's like a charm-

ing white knight, coming to your rescue when you need it the most... wielding your bra instead of a sword?

Enough said! She headed back inside and set herself up in her first-floor office. The distance giving her the quiet she needed, but the window giving her ample view of the garden. While her office was barren, a solitary plant on her white desk the only splash of colour against the unpacked boxes, bare floors and stripped walls, outside was a scene of joyous colour.

And that joy had her smiling as she opened up her laptop.

She may not have the entire summer covered, but she had the immediate future taken care of, and that was miracle enough.

Not that Porsha believed in miracles or fairy godmothers or heavenly forces like guardian angels. But even she had to admit, this was up there with them all.

Matteo the Manny, her saviour and one *extremely hot* white knight.

CHAPTER TWO

MATTEO WATCHED HER GO, questioning not his offer of helping to look after Fin but his innate need to make her laugh, to blush, to bring some colourful relief to her otherwise grave persona.

And he had questions, so many questions.

Why was the boy with her? Where were his parents if she was his aunt? Why the brief shadow of sorrow when she'd spoken of her family? What had happened with the nanny? And why did she have a persistent crease between her brows? She couldn't be more than thirty, so it wasn't through age...

'You ready, Lucky?'

'Born ready.'

He turned back to Fin and dusted off his hands. Crouching down, he primed himself for a goal save, though his mind was still abuzz with her.

'What happened with Ms Smith?' he asked as he saved Fin's goal and rolled the ball back. 'She didn't look too happy...'

The boy screwed up his face. 'She always looked like a bulldog chewing a bee.'

Matteo chuckled. 'A wasp. It's "a bulldog chewing a wasp."'

The boy shrugged. '"Bulldog, bee" sound better.'

'I won't argue with that.'

Matteo waited for Fin to take his next kick, a sweet shot tight to the plant pot-cum-goal post. 'Nice!' He rolled it back, crouched down. 'So, you didn't do anything to upset her?'

Another shrug. 'I didn't mean to get paint on her *precious* bag, but she did put it on the table.'

'I see.'

'And I didn't mean to pour milk on her phone, but my hand slipped.'

'Right.'

'And it was *her* fault her glasses ended up in the bin.' He struck the ball hard and missed the goal. 'She was the one who asked me to clear the table after breakfast, and they got scooped up.'

'All that, hey?' Matteo retrieved the ball and rolled it back to him. 'And the fact she was soaking wet when she left…?'

'She got in the way of my target practice.'

'With the bombs?'

Fin nodded, eyes evading Matteo as he rocked the ball back and forth under his foot, suddenly subdued and Matteo regretted prying. 'Fin, it's—'

'If I tell you something,' the boy interrupted, glancing up, 'will you promise not to tell Aunt Porsha?'

Matteo frowned, taken aback. 'That depends on

what it is. If it's something I think she needs to know, I'd have to tell her.'

He flicked the ball up into his arms and stepped closer, his young brow furrowed. 'The truth is, I don't like it when they're here. I like it when it's me and Aunt Porsha. She works too hard. Like *all* the time. And I figured, if she has to look after me instead, then she won't have to work so much.'

'So you think making the babysitter leave—'

'I'm not a baby! I don't need *baby*sitting!'

'Good point. The nanny—'

'That doesn't sound much better.'

'Child minder?' He couldn't believe he was negotiating job titles with a—

'How old are you?'

Fin cocked his head. 'Why?'

'Since we're discussing an appropriate title for the adult in charge of you…'

'I'm seven and three-quarters.'

Matteo raised his brows, gave an impressed whistle. 'That old. Okay, child minder it is… So you think by getting the child minders to quit, you'll be forcing your aunt to work less?'

'And play with me more.' Fin's eyes brightened, clearly pleased to have him catch on so quick. 'Yes.'

Matteo chuckled. Oh, to be a child again. 'If only it were that simple, kid.'

Fin frowned. 'It isn't?'

'I hate to burst your bubble, but I take it there's

no uncle, so your aunt and you are alone in this big house, and that belly of yours needs food in it. All of which requires money, and to get money your aunt needs to work.'

'But how can I get an uncle if all my aunt does is work?'

And that's the bit the boy chose to focus on? Matteo shook his head, realising he was fighting a losing battle. In Fin's simple world, the simple made sense. 'You got me, kid.'

'When I'm older, I'll work hard so she doesn't have to.'

Matteo gave a weighted huff. Fin's declaration, the exact promise he'd made himself when he was of a similar age. Swearing to earn enough so that his mother could stop working all the hours. Earn enough so that she could smile more, eat better, live richer.

He'd succeeded too...not that she was still alive to enjoy it.

'That's a good goal to have. But for now, how about some tricks?'

'I know a lot of tricks.'

Fin's blue eyes glittered with mischief, and Matteo laughed.

'I meant football tricks. Like the stepover?'

'Sounds a bit rubbish, that?'

Matteo flicked the ball up and demonstrated it with effortless ease, getting around Fin before the boy knew which way to look. 'Wow, neat!'

'Now it's your turn. Follow what I do…'

And so he did. Fin watched intently, doing as Matteo did, until he was asking to learn another and another. Matteo obliged. Repeatedly. Running through a skill set that he had learnt as a boy. And it was exhilarating, doing what he loved with a child who obviously loved it too. Losing track of time in the raw enjoyment of it.

No pressure, just fun.

'You'll have to teach me that one…'

They turned to find Porsha in the doorway. 'Sorry, I didn't see you there.'

Something about her eyes caught at him. A wistfulness that had him scooping up the ball and stepping closer, the urge to make her smile returning. 'You been there long?'

'Long enough.' She smiled—*Hurrah*—but it melted just as quick. 'I'm sorry I was gone so long.'

'You were?' Matteo checked his watch. Almost two hours had passed, and he'd barely noticed. 'Wow, so you were. How was the meeting?'

'It could have gone better.'

'But it could have gone a lot worse?' he countered.

'True.' The tiny smile made a comeback. 'It's hard dealing with crises over Zoom, harder to gauge the room, so to speak.'

He got that. He preferred to be on the ground when a development project hit a snag. 'Where's your office based?'

'Canary Wharf.'

'So, why aren't you…? Ah, of course.' He flicked a look at Fin, who'd managed to grapple the ball from him unaware and was practising what he'd learnt. 'No childcare options at your place of work?'

She laughed. 'My boss would see that as the worst possible distraction, and even if there were, Fin would have seen himself evicted by now.' She grimaced. 'Not that he deserves it, just that…well, he's a handful.'

'Not to me he isn't.'

'That's sweet of you say, but I can take it from here. I really ought to think about getting dinner on, getting Fin settled, and then I can get back to it.'

She was watching Fin rather than him, and he could sense her brain working overtime with whatever dregs of the day she had to wrap up.

'Tell you what. Why doesn't Fin come to mine?'

Her eyes snapped to his. Wide.

'I have plenty to keep him busy while you finish up, and then *I'll* sort dinner for the three of us.'

'No—no, I couldn't possibly put you out more than I already have.'

'You forget, I've enjoyed this afternoon as much as he has. Whereas you, on the other hand, look like you have the weight of the world on your shoulders. Get work wrapped up. Get yourself freshened up.' She touched a self-conscious hand to her hair, and he cursed his choice of words, bit back the compliment that wanted to follow and said, 'It'll be my pleasure to cook for more than one for a change.'

'I don't know...'

'Please, Aunt Porsha!' Fin burst in, overhearing the offer. 'Please, pretty please!'

'It really is no problem. He can check out the pool too and—'

'You have a *pool*?' Fin's eyes returned to their bugged out state while Porsha's cheeks paled.

'In the basement, yeah.' Matteo was saying it for Fin's benefit, but his eyes were caught in Porsha's. The surprising horror, the green tinge to her cheeks...

'That is so cool, I'm—'

'Not today, okay?' Porsha touched a blind hand to Fin's shoulder. 'Sorry. I'm just—' She wet her lips, hesitated, and Matteo's racing mind explained it for her.

You're a single male, no kids of your own, and you're inviting hers over. What would you do in her position?

'Sorry, that—'

'Would you—?' she said at the same time.

'You go,' he said.

She smiled, though it struggled to mask what he'd already witnessed. 'I was going to ask if you'd mind staying here instead?'

'Of course,' he rushed out, grateful for the lifeline. 'I'm not entirely sure what food we have, but we could order a takeaway,' she suggested. 'It can be my thank-you for today.'

'No takeaway necessary. Fin and I will rustle something up together.'

She gave a chuckle, the breezy tinkle seeing off the dregs of tension.

'I can already envision the chaos.'

'No chaos, only fun.'

'Speaking from experience…'

'You did tell me to whisk the eggs, Aunt Porsha,' Fin grumbled from somewhere between them.

'Not on full blast, I didn't.'

Now it was Matteo who laughed, picturing the scene in all its messy glory.

'I don't know how to thank you for this…' She blinked up at him, all soft and sincere, and what he wouldn't give to be on the receiving end of that look daily, if not hourly. 'It really is very sweet of you.'

He cleared his throat, trademark grin in place. 'Just don't tell the world. I have a reputation to maintain.'

She shook her head and laughed in one. Happy yet incredulous. And he couldn't blame her. This wasn't how he'd seen his day going either.

'Any dietary requirements I should know about?'

'No. We're pretty straightforward.'

He got the impression they were far from straight-forward, but he wasn't about to say as much.

'Excellent.'

'And you're really sure you don't mind doing this?'

'Not in the slightest.'

'Do you want me to show you around the kitchen?'

'No need. I've got Fin to do that.'

'But—'

'*Go*, Porsha.'

'Okay, I'll just be upstairs…' she waved a hand behind her '…if you need anything. Anything at all.'

'We won't. But if we do…' he conceded.

'I'll see you later then.'

'You will.'

With that she turned and walked, glancing back midway to the house. Was she checking he was still there? He waved and she gave a quick smile before picking up her pace.

Yup, definitely checking he was still there, just as Matteo was triple checking he was for real too. Childminding to cooking…*cazzo,* next he'd be offering to clean!

CHAPTER THREE

PORSHA CLOSED HER laptop and stood, stretching off her back as it bemoaned the previous three hours hunched over her desk.

She wasn't done—she never was—but the sun was calling it a day and so should she.

Leaving her office, she followed the scent on the air…

Had her house ever smelt so delicious?

She ran her fingers through her hair, wishing she'd thought to brush it first, but she'd left them to it long enough, and guilt was riding as high as her nerves.

And she didn't get nervous. She was the unemotional one, the one people came to when *they* were nervous and wanted calming down. But then, she had never been one for chasing someone out her front door smelling of sweet desperation either. What a display!

She hated to admit it, but she wasn't…well, she wasn't herself any more.

And it was one thing to trust a neighbour with that responsibility, another to trust someone with world-renowned fame and the ability to make her stomach somersault with the smallest of looks. She'd been concerned she hadn't been in her right mind when she agreed to let Matteo look after Fin, so she'd hit the internet between meetings and phone calls, gleaning all she could.

Everything, from his football fame to his love life—TMI in the extreme—to his patchy childhood history. Growing up in a troubled London suburb with his Italian grandparents and single mother, he'd been going off the rails when he'd been spotted by a scout for a Premier League club and his career had taken off.

He was the kind of real-life fairy-tale the press loved to print about. Coming from little and making himself into a lot. *A lot, a lot.* Investing his earnings in property from a very young age, and making a name for himself in that world too.

And she was no fool. She may have done well for herself, climbing the corporate ladder to heights she'd once thought out of her reach, but he was on a different stratosphere.

Yet here he was, in *her* home. Though as she stepped into the unbelievably tidy kitchen, table made for two, her scented candle lit in the middle, she might as well have stepped into a parallel universe. One where this was his home—*their home*, even.

'Hey.' Matteo looked up from the hob, ever more breathtaking in his ever more homely role.

How was it possible he could look even better after hours of childcare and cooking when she'd look—well, she'd look like she did now. Hair askew, frown lines deep from squinting at her screen, the minimal make-up she'd applied that morning worn away.

'Hi.' She smoothed her palms down her black jeans, straightened out her blouse. 'You found everything, then?'

'I did.' He grinned as he stirred the pan. 'Fin made an excellent sous-chef, he even laid the table.'

'A table for two?' she said looking at it and realising its meaning. 'Are you not…?'

And you shouldn't be sad about it! The man has a life to get back to next door!

'Ah…' The way he said it had her eyes launching back to his. 'I have a confession to make.'

'You do?' Her pulse hitched.

'I might have fed him earlier.'

'Oh!' *And breathe.* 'You did? So this is…'

'For us, yes. Is that okay?'

'Of course!' She smothered her squeak of a response with a smile. 'I can hardly kick you out before you get to enjoy what you've made.'

She was *trying* to make it sound perfectly fine but feared her nerves were winning out. Scratching at a non-existent itch behind her ear, she glanced around the room.

'Speaking of Fin, where is he?'

Because, boy, did she need him here.

'And that brings me to my next confession…'

Her heart swooped anew. 'Why—what's happened?'

'Nothing bad, don't worry,' he rushed out, coming towards her as he sensed her panic. 'But he's spark out—from tiredness not a ball to the head! I promise. I fed him and…'

He led her back into the hall and cocked his head towards the family room. He lifted a finger to his lips. Lips she really shouldn't be focusing on when her nephew was her priority.

She padded forward and peeped inside, letting go of a faint breath at the sight that welcomed her. One of the few rooms finished, it had been designed with Fin in mind. Space for board games and movies, snacks and snuggles, and right now, he was most definitely snuggling.

Fast asleep on the plush grey sofa that hugged one corner of the room, a blanket pulled up to his chin, cheeks a healthy pink. The TV on one wall played quietly while a game of chess rested on the pouffe in front of him—*chess*!

She stifled a surprised laugh. She'd inadvertently inherited the board from an ex many moons ago, and it hadn't seen the light of day since.

'He asked to have a go,' Matteo whispered, spying her focus.

'At *chess*?'

He nodded. 'Though he did fall asleep not long in… I figured it was best to let him rest.'

She smiled, eased back out of the room. 'I'm not sure what's more surprising, Fin asking to play it or you actually…'

She pressed her lips together.

He raised his brows. 'Or me…?'

'Nothing.'

'You can say it.'

She looked away, swallowing the chaotic fluttering in her chest. 'It doesn't strike me as the sort of game to hold a footballer's attention.'

'How so?'

She chanced a glance his way, saw how his mouth twitched and his eyes danced and responded in kind.

'Not enough action.'

'Ah, well, that depends on who's playing…'

Something about the way he said it—all husky and low—had her body combusting. Was strip chess a thing? And why on earth had her brain travelled down that road?

'Chess and football actually have a lot in common…it's all about position and strategy.'

She nodded. Position. There were so many positions she wanted to be in with him this second, and she swore she gave another squeak when she swallowed.

'You're right though, it's not something I ever really played before I quit the field…'

He eased back but the damage was done, every inch of her on fire for him.

'I'm in a phase of trying new things, and of my newfound interests, this is the one my therapist insists I do more of—' He broke off with a sudden cough. 'And that was too much information for a first date. You hungry?'

She gawped. Unsure what startled her more, the mention of a therapist or a date…

'Not that this is a date!' he rushed out. 'Hell, I'm really messing this up, aren't I?'

'No, of course not!'

And then she laughed with him. His unease taking the edge off her own, thankfully taking the edge off the heat too. It was much easier being around the great Lucky Luca when he wasn't quite so composed himself.

As for the therapist—who was he seeing and why?

She wanted to ask. And not just because she'd left Fin with him. She cared. She wanted to be there for him, like he'd been there for her that day. Ease his burden, too.

As for the newfound interests he mentioned, was he referring to the kind that saw the press printing the phrase 'death wish' in his name too many times to count?

She'd seen pictures too. Of daredevil stunts and death-defying activities that lifted the hairs on her arms.

Was he running from himself, looking for a new high to fill the hole football had left, struggling with his new reality?

'So…' he cocked his head '…you hungry?'

'Ravenous.'

She made a mental note to raise it when the time felt right, because now wasn't it. Not when she genuinely was ravenous, and he was so eager to feed her.

She gave Fin one last look and followed Matteo back into the kitchen, but she wasn't quite ready to sit at the table for two. It looked far too intimate and cosy, the soft glow from the candle making the butterflies within her have butterflies themselves.

'I hope you don't mind that I fed Fin earlier?' Matteo asked, pulling two empty bowls out of the oven.

Pre-warming the dishes? Porsha couldn't believe her eyes. She never thought to—or rather, never had the time for such luxury.

'Not at all.'

'He was starving.'

She laughed. 'He's always starving.'

'He's a growing boy.'

He stirred the pan once more, and the scent rising on the steam had her stepping closer, her stomach rumbling as it registered tomato, garlic, herbs… Fresh bread, too?

'Whatever you're cooking, it smells delicious.'

'It's chicken cacciatore with a De Luca twist.'

'What's the twist?'

'Now that's a family secret…if I told you I'd have to kill you. Or keep you locked up in my basement. Your choice.'

His eyes danced, his tease provoking her playful spirit, which didn't get an outing often.

'Considering your basement houses a pool, that would be an easy decision to make.'

And now she was thinking of being in her swimsuit in his space, him in his trunks, and that really wasn't helping either. She may not like the water, but if it stripped off his layers…

'Wine?' he asked.

'Please!' She dived on the suggestion. 'Though I'll get it, you're cooking.'

'It's okay, I'm already on it. Red, white, champagne?'

'Whatever you're having is fine with me. Wait, I don't have any—'

He looked sheepish. 'You didn't have a lot of stuff, so I sent a courier.'

'Matteo!'

'What?' His eyes were wide with forced innocence, and by his charm-filled grin he knew he'd get away with it too.

'And I thought Fin was the incorrigible one.'

'That boy is awesome.'

'I know.'

He plucked a bottle of red out of the cupboard

where all her drinks were kept, gifting her a glimpse of her shelves that looked considerably fuller than they were before. 'Now, take a seat and I'll bring it over.'

She settled herself at the table, fighting the urge to blow out the candle and the ambience with it.

You've got this, Porsha. It's just dinner with your neighbour. No more. No less.

She focused on her breathing rather than the elevated rate of her pulse. Adjusted her blouse. Checked her nails. Sneaked a look at him from beneath her lashes as he approached, wine now open and ready to be poured.

Still in his shorts and T shirt he wasn't dressed date-worthy, which should calm her. Only it didn't, because he could walk down the street wearing nothing more than a bin bag and be considered designer in every way.

Sexy too.

Though Matteo in a bin bag…

'What's that smile about?' he said as he filled her wine glass.

Her eyes leapt to his. *Keep your cool.*

'If I tell you, I'd have to kill you—' she took up the drink he'd poured for her '—or lock you in my basement, and that room isn't getting renovated for a long time yet, so…' Shrug '…your choice.'

Proud of her rebuke and the laugh he gave, she took a sip of her wine and sighed. It was warm and fruity and just what she needed. She also liked making him laugh. It wasn't often people laughed in her presence. If anything, she was considered the serious and severe one. Serious, severe, sensible…all up there with *stoic*.

'Is it okay?' he asked.

'It's lovely.' She took another much-needed sip. 'Thank you.'

He held her gaze a second longer, long enough to have her cheeks warming again. At this rate she would have to start wearing foundation in his company just to tone down her beacon-like head.

'It's a good job you're hungry' he said, returning to the hob and ladling out the food. 'When I said I wasn't used to cooking for more than one, I meant it. It looks like I'm feeding the five thousand and then some.'

'Do you really not entertain much?'

She found it hard to believe after all she'd read on his extensive social life…

'To be honest, I'm the one getting entertained most of the time…hotels, restaurants, award ceremonies, galas, you name it, I've done it. But cooking for others, not so much.'

'You enjoy it though?'

He smiled. 'Is it that obvious?'

'You're very at home in the kitchen, and when it smells as good as this, it suggests you do…'

'I think it's more indicative of having too much time on my hands of late.'

She held her tongue as the questions rose with

her concern. What did he do now? Could property development ever fill the hole left by his first love—football?

In all those articles she'd read, one was a passion, the other was a necessity. He made no bones about it.

Property was the career to see him through long after the game had ended. But surely the kind of passion someone like Matteo had for the sport, the passion she could see spilling over when he was playing with Fin, didn't just end. There had to be a more natural evolution for him. One that moved from playing the sport to teaching it, commentating on it, doing something with it, anything other than dealing purely in property?

Though to have a secondary income of that magnitude was impressive. It showed prudence. Foresight. Sensible traits she could get on board with.

'Buon appetito!'

He placed a bowl in front of her, the scent of the rich red sauce making her mouth water. A family secret he had said…

'Thank you.' She placed her napkin over her lap and waited for him to sit before asking, 'Did your mother teach you the recipe?'

She regretted the question as soon as it was out. The tension it triggered, the way his eyes flickered as he took a swig of his wine.

'No. My grandmother.'

There was no love, no warmth, no wistful look in his eye…

She tried for a smile. 'Well, I'm sure you've done her justice.'

'You'll have to taste it and let me know.'

Though his expression didn't lift. The aloof mask more concerning than her empty stomach. Was he trying to bury his grief?

Something she was having to do daily.

Did it still affect him so…?

She'd read about the loss of his mother seven years ago. His grandparents shortly before that. But as she was swiftly learning, grief didn't come with an expiry date.

She could press or she could let it go. If she pressed, she risked upsetting him further. And that was the last thing she wanted to do. So she added it to the mental note for later and did as he asked—tasted his food. And *oh my*, was it good! Her blissful moan, no fake.

'*Bene?*'

She covered her mouth, nodding over the taste explosion. The man really did know how to cook.

'*Molto bene.*'

His eyes widened. 'You speak Italian?'

She laughed, almost choking on the remnants. 'I wish. I'm afraid that's my lot. That and *si*. And I can throw in a *ciao* too.'

'And a *no*.'

'No?'

'*No* is no.'

'Oh, right! Yes! *Sí!*'

They both laughed. And for a moment she just enjoyed it. Forgetting all else but the delicious meal and the equally delicious company. When was the last time she'd conversed with an adult outside of work?

It felt nice. The silence that fell between them easy.

Silence. Something else she wasn't used to. Fin could talk his way through every bite, multitasking at its finest.

'I hope Fin was good for you.'

Usually she winced or didn't ask at all for fear of what the other person would say, but Matteo smiled that lazy grin of his, and the knot between her shoulders eased.

'*Molto bene,*' he said.

She raised one cynical brow. Was he using the same Italian phrase to tease? To mask the truth?

'Seriously, Porsha, he was very good. No trouble at all.'

'No accidental mishaps? No mini fires? No flying underwear?'

He chuckled, the low rumble and spark to his eyes lighting her up inside.

'No, much to my disappointment. We played more football. Did some sprint work. Got cleaned up. Cooked. He ate. Then learnt the move of every chess piece before falling asleep.'

She nodded slowly.

'You don't believe me?'

'I'm letting it sink in.'

He took up his wine, not once releasing her from his gaze. There was something he wasn't saying…something about Fin…

'You can say it.'

'Say what?'

'That he's a monkey.'

He huffed on a smile. 'A monkey?'

'In the mischievous sense…'

'He's a good kid.'

She bristled. 'I didn't say he wasn't.'

'But you worry that he isn't?'

She took a breath. She'd snapped and it wasn't his fault. He was being sweet and kind, and she was edgy. All because he was better with Fin than she was, better in the kitchen too judging by this meal…not to mention his voice made her pulse spike, his grin made her knees weak, and his kindness…his kindness…

Breathe, Porsha!

'I worry that I can't keep a nanny long enough to keep my sanity.'

He considered her for a long moment.

'Then maybe it's time to explore other avenues of childcare?'

'I've explored *all* the avenues bar boarding school, and I refuse to send him away. He's been through enough.'

His eyes softened. 'I get that.'

'You do?' Because how could he, unless… 'He told you about my—my sister? His mum.'

She took up her glass though she didn't drink. Didn't think she could get it past the wedge that had formed.

'He told me she died in an accident…'

Goosebumps prickled all over her body. Her stomach plummeted. An accident. Oh, how she hated that word—*accident*—the images it would throw up…the nightmares it would trigger.

'What—what did he tell you?'

'That was all he said, and I didn't press. But to have her here one minute and gone the next, for you as well… I'm sorry, I didn't mean to upset you.'

'I know.' Because she did and time had moved on, though her grief… 'It was two years ago, but it…it's hard to come to terms with.'

'It's gonna take time. And even then, pain like that never really dies. It evolves but never goes away. I only said it so that you'd know he'd told me, that I understand a little of what you've both been through and how devastating it must have been.'

Was he talking of his own loss? His mother? His grandparents? There was no aloofness now. His eyes were filled with compassion as she wrestled with her pain. The cruelty and chaos of life. To end her sister's when she'd been so young. To send her own on such a pivotal twist. To leave her floundering…

'Which is why I hope you'll consider letting me help you, just until you can find a more permanent arrangement.'

'What?' She hauled herself out of the fog. 'You can't be saying…?'

'I'm saying I can step in until you can sort out childcare that you're both happy with.'

'No, Matteo, I couldn't—' She shook her head, struggling to believe the words coming out of his mouth. If she'd thought the situation surreal before, now she had to be dreaming.

'Please, Porsha. I want to help.'

'But it could be days, weeks even. And it's the summer holidays, five days a week.'

'A summer arrangement then…? If it makes you happier to give it an end date. You're long overdue a break, or so your nephew tells me.'

'He's seven!'

'And he's seen enough.'

Had she really been that stressed around him? That tired?

'I try not to let it show.'

'I'm sure you do, and he couldn't be in better hands.'

He could. He could be in Matteo's. And that's exactly what the man was offering her. The answer to her summer prayers and one that was sure to bring Fin so much joy.

'Can I think about it? I don't mean to sound ungrateful but…'

'Of course, and while you're thinking, I'll be here.'

He gave her that reassuring smile that made her want to nestle against his chest and have him hold her. And where had that thought come from? She didn't depend on anyone for that kind of comfort. Not ever.

'Can I ask you something though?'

The way he said it had her shoulders bunching. 'Yes?'

'You don't need to tell me, but…he didn't mention his father. And with him being left with you, I assume…'

She nibbled her lip, contemplating how best to say it and realising there wasn't one.

'My little sister isn't—wasn't like me. She was very young when she had him, barely an adult herself, and she didn't take her role as a mother seriously…she didn't take *anything* seriously. She was more about seeing the world, living each day as it comes. She often left Fin with our parents so that she didn't have to change the way she lived…'

'And his father?'

She cleared her throat. 'I don't know. I don't think she knew.'

'Where he is or didn't know who…'

'Like I said, she was a free spirit in every sense of the word.'

His brows lifted. 'So, his father could be anyone?'

'Anywhere.'

He shook his head slowly, eyes turning inward. 'It seems Fin and I have a lot in common.'

'You don't know who your…'

She didn't need to finish, the grim set of his mouth, the hard edge to his eyes told her all she needed to know.

'I know enough to know that I don't want to know.'

And for that, maybe he understood Fin better than she ever would.

'I'm sorry you went through that too. It can't be easy growing up without a father.'

'Where I come from in Italy, it is the worst mistake you can make. To get pregnant, not just out of wedlock but at the age my mother did. I brought shame on my entire family.'

'You mean the situation, not you. You were the innocent in—'

'Not in the eyes of my grandparents.' His tone brooked no argument. 'They were forced to leave the village where their family had lived for generations. They came to London to escape the judgement of others, but they never really escaped their own. My mother and I certainly never escaped it.'

Porsha's heart wept for the boy he had been, his young mother too. None of this had come across in the fluff pieces she had read.

'I can't imagine how hard that must have been

for you both. Growing up in that environment…'
She shivered. 'They should have been protecting
you, loving you.'

'*Certamente*. But they didn't. And I did what
any kid would when faced with such adversity, I
acted up, made their lives hell, but in so doing I
made my mother's hell too.'

She could hear the self-loathing in his voice,
see it in his eyes.

'But you were hurting.'

'I was, but I didn't understand that at the time.
I only knew that my grandparents resented my
presence, and my mother was caught in the middle. She was suffering and I made it worse. So
much worse.'

'You were a kid.'

He lifted one stiffened shoulder. 'It's no excuse.
I hate what I put her through, the extra worry I
caused her. If football hadn't come along when it
had, I'm not sure where I'd be. Probably prison.'

She shook her head. 'You're too good for that.'

A faint smile touched his lips. 'There are plenty
of lost souls in prison who weren't lucky enough
to be found.'

'That's what you put it down to, your success,
luck at being found? Not the hard work you put
in? The blood, sweat and tears it must have taken
to get to the heights you did.'

He chuckled, pressing back in his seat. 'No,
there was plenty of that too.'

'I read about your football coach…' She pressed her lips together on her blunder. Worried how he would take it.

'Been reading up on me?'

'I did leave Fin with you,' she hurried to say, hoping it would be explanation enough. 'I'd hardly be doing my duty to him if I hadn't at least done a cursory check.'

'That's true,' he said, taking a sip of his wine, his eyes reading hers. Wanting to know what she thought of all she'd read, she was sure.

'Besides—' she gave him a coy smile '—I felt like I was the only person in the world not to know who you were.'

'And how pleasant and refreshing that was. Even if it was but for a moment…'

She blushed further. 'I'm not saying I believe everything I read, especially the more…'

'Fruity?' he provided for her.

She gave an amused huff, reached for her wine. 'I was going to say "personal," but yes, "fruity" works.'

'You think my personal life *fruity*?'

She choked on her drink. 'You put it out there!'

'And I'm asking if you agree?'

His eyes were hot, unashamed as they burned into hers, refusing to let go.

Oh, heaven help me!

Everything within her had come alive, heat unfurling low in her abdomen, a tension that promised such release pulling her body taut. She wet her lips, willing it to dissipate, but it only made his eyes dip to the move, their depths speaking of the same.

'That would depend on how much of it was true,' she said, breathless.

'I would say most of it. Embellished for sure, but mostly true.'

She swallowed the nervous leap to her heart and gave a smile worthy of his boldness. 'How exhausting that must have been for you...*all* those women to satisfy *and* all those footie fans too.'

For a second he didn't react, not even to blink, and then he laughed. And didn't stop.

'Oh, Porsha, you are fun. Truly fun.'

Was she? She sat straighter, felt an invisible hand pat her on the back—*See, you're not the boring workaholic everyone has you pegged for.*

'Coach would have *loved* you.'

'Which coach?'

'The one who found me.' He topped up her wine glass, his smile filled with fondness now. 'I guess you could say he was the father figure I never had. He worked me so hard most days I was too tired to think about what mischief I could cause. Too tired to hang out with my usual crowd too.'

'And that was a good thing?'

'With the steadily growing number of criminal records among us—very. It was only a matter of time before I landed one.'

'So, you traded the underworld for football?'

'You could say that. I lived and breathed the sport from sunup until sundown. Even at school my head was on the game, my feet itching to get back out on the field. It was everything to me.'

She chewed her lip, appreciating his honesty and wanting more. The time felt right to ask for it too.

'And what about now? Now that you're retired?'

She sensed the cold seeping back into his body, saw the darkness come over his expression. He didn't look like the self-assured, world-renowned footballer and notorious playboy any more. He looked like the lost boy of his youth, and her chest ached for him.

'Now I'm having to re-evaluate what everything is…'

CHAPTER FOUR

HOW IN THE hell had they got to this point?

Matteo had told Porsha what it had taken his therapist several very expensive and very uncomfortable sessions to drag out of him.

'I can't imagine what that must feel like,' she murmured, soft and soothing, full of understanding. Understanding that had his throat closing over.

He wanted the focus off him before he said anything else, *did* anything else foolish.

'I don't know…' He took up his glass, needing the warmth of the wine to take out the chill. 'Seems you found yourself in a similar boat two years ago, forcing you to reevaluate your priorities and the way you live. It can't have been easy fitting a child into your life.'

Her nostrils flared as she stared back at him, pain swirling in her honeyed depths. And now he felt like an arse. A complete and utter arse. Detracting from his pain by launching headlong into hers. 'I'm sorry, I shouldn't have said…'

'No, you're right. It did change my life. Over-night, I lost a sister and gained a child. It was…it was as life-altering as you can imagine, but my parents helped in the beginning. They were al-ways quick to drop everything for Fin and—and Sassy.'

'Sassy?'

'My sister.'

'Of course.' *Idiot.*

'If Fin spent so much time with your parents before, how did he end up with you?'

He winced as she stiffened. *Dio*, why was he so bad at this?

'That came out wrong. What I mean is…from what you've said about your sister, she doesn't strike me as the type to write a will, and yet you're the one who's taken on sole responsibility for him, not them.'

'I'm his godmother. It wasn't up for debate. Not in my eyes.'

'So, your sister chose you?'

Tears filled her eyes, tugging at his chest as she smiled. 'I guess she did.'

'But you doubt her choice?'

'No. God no. I'm far better placed to give him a stable home life.'

Stable. A word he sensed held so much mean-ing for her.

'Yet you're hesitant about it? You didn't say "she did." You said, "I guess she did."'

'It's been difficult, that's all. Coping with her loss, trying to find a new routine that works. Both at home and at work. My parents watched him for me in the early days, when we were all struggling with the shock and trying to keep it together for Fin.'

'Your company gave you leave though?'

'Yes. But then I was going out of my mind, worrying about the future, how I was going to make it work. Fin living with me, my job, my home, my parents buzzing about. They offered to take him on their travels with them—can you imagine?'

Matteo gave a noncommittal shake of his head because he couldn't. He had no idea what they were like. But Porsha clearly had a strong opinion on it.

'Travel sounds like an exciting thing to do as a child.'

'Not when it takes precedence over school.'

'Ah…' Yes, he could totally see her having something to say about that.

'And besides, they were itching to get back to it. The roads were calling…'

'They said so?' Sounded a bit insensitive to him, but then what did he know of true parenting? His mother's had been a browbeaten affair courtesy of his ever-present grandparents.

'No. Of course not. But I could tell. And I figured the sooner they got back to their way of living, the sooner we could find a new way of living for us. Get into a routine. Fin had been so up and down, challenging, angry…understandably. And I don't think my parents made for the best example. In their view, *all* emotions are for expressing as deeply and as loudly as possible. None of that stiff-upper-lip nonsense.'

'There's something healthy in that…'

Ha! Have you heard yourself? Do as I say, not as I do. Ring a bell?

'There is. But not to the extent they go about it. Social norms are for others to conform to. They're too restrictive and destructive to our creativity. Clothing is as optional as school—honestly!' she stressed when he raised a brow. 'They're as hippy as you can get for the twenty-first century. And I wanted him to have some normality. Figured he was craving it. That some of his behavioural issues came down to their idiosyncrasies.'

'So you told them you didn't need them any more?'

'I told them we'd be okay, that I had it covered and that they should follow their dreams again. They were set to do Route 66 for Dad's sixtieth when Sassy announced she was pregnant. And after that…well, they didn't dare go anywhere in case Sassy—or rather Fin—needed them.'

'So you packed them off under the pretence of letting them get back to it, but in reality you thought it best for him?'

She hesitated, lowering her lashes as she looked

to the table rather than him. Was she questioning her decision? The assumptions she had made about what her parents wanted and what she thought was best for Fin too.

'It wasn't all a pretence...'

'But it must have been a while ago... Are they not back, ready to lend a hand again?'

Though he knew the answer well enough, else he wouldn't be here now.

'They come back occasionally.'

'They're *still* travelling?'

She gave an awkward laugh. 'I think they're in Slovenia, on route to Croatia right about now.'

His brows lifted. 'Nice.'

'It is nice...'

'But?'

She shrugged. 'There is no "but".'

'So, they're happy to leave you for extended periods, but they weren't so happy to leave Sassy to it?'

'They trust me.' And then she winced. Realising what she'd admitted to in that same breath. 'But then I've always been the sensible one, the responsible one. Not just out of me and Sassy but them too. They trust me to be okay and therefore Fin.'

'And are you? Okay, I mean.'

She blinked across the table at him. Was that surprise? Shock? The suppression of more tears...?

He wanted to reach out and squeeze her hand,

tell her she had this when, really, her parents should have been the ones to do it. He was no more than a stranger, a neighbour with a deep-rooted desire to help…

She sipped at her wine, her delicate throat bobbing as she swallowed.

'You've asked me that more than once today.'

'Is that a problem?'

'It's not a question I'm used to hearing.'

'No, I can see that…doesn't mean I'll let you go without answering.'

She gave the ghost of a smile. 'I'm doing my best to be.'

It wasn't effusive. But it was the truth.

'Now that Fin's with me, I intend to give him the stability he lacked in his early years. I intend to let my parents live their life again and see to it that he gets to live his with as little disruption as possible.'

'That's very noble.'

She snorted. 'It's less about nobility and more about duty. My sister entrusted him to me, and I don't want to let her down. Or him.'

'That would never happen.'

Her downcast gaze told him she thought differently.

'You worry that it might?'

'I worry that I'm hardly Mother of the Year material.'

'What makes you say that?'

She set her cutlery aside, food forgotten as the conversation took over.

'I wasn't ready for children.' She took an uneasy breath, her gaze drifting to the garden outdoors. 'I'm still not.'

'Okay,' he said cautiously, 'you're young, it stands to reason that—'

'I'm twenty-seven.'

'So you would have been twenty-five when it happened. It's okay that you weren't ready, that you're still not now…'

'But it's not okay, is it?' She turned back to him, eyes wide. 'Because now I have one, and I feel like I'm failing him every day.'

'Because you don't think you're ready?'

'Because *look* at me, look at my life! It wasn't designed for a boy to come tearing through it. My house is mid-renovation, half of it is uninhabitable, the garden is tiny, and my work leaves little time for much else.'

It tore from her lips, one word tripping over the next, as though she'd had it trapped inside for months…twenty-four to be exact.

'So change it.'

'Why should I?' She bit her lip. 'I'm sorry, I don't mean that.'

'You do, else you wouldn't have said it.'

She rubbed a weary hand across her brow, leaning her elbow into the table.

'It's okay to say it, Porsha. To feel it.'

He wanted to get up from his seat, round the table and massage her shoulders until they were no longer hunched about her ears.

'It's not,' she whispered, easing back in her chair as her eyes met his once more. 'Not really. But the thing is, my sister and I, we didn't have the most orthodox of upbringings. She was the way she was because she was just like them. Carefree. Wild. Irresponsible. Passionate with their love but flighty in all else. We travelled around a lot, rarely staying in one place longer than a year. It was a challenge to get an education, let alone a decent one. And the more difficult they made it, the harder I worked. I was determined to break away as soon as I could and set down roots, take control of my life.'

'Which you are doing?'

'Yes. Or I was trying to… One day, I figured I'd meet the right man to share that responsibility with. Someone who I could trust to have a child with. Who would value that stability too. But right now, there's just me and a house that isn't fit to be called a home.'

'I think you place too much stock in stuff.'

She frowned. 'How do you mean?'

He shrugged. 'You've put a roof over his head, food on the table, and you've given him a home even if you don't see it as one yet. And every day you love him. That's all he needs.'

She chewed her cheek, said nothing.

'From where I'm sitting, Porsha, you're doing everything you can to give him a loving stable home life.'

'That's what I want, what I'm striving for, but—' she choked on a laugh '—I feel the least stable I've ever been.'

'You're on a steep learning curve. Having a baby is hard enough, having a child come to you at the age of—what?—five? Suffering the grief you must have been going through. Both of you. It would be weird if you *were* stable.'

'But as the responsible adult, you don't get to crack.'

'Who says?'

'Me.' She pressed a palm to her chest. 'I say.'

He stared at her long and hard. 'You get to be human too.'

He hadn't hated his mum when she'd broken down in front of him. No, he'd only hated his grandparents more.

'You also get to take a break occasionally, get some real downtime.'

'Downtime?' She shook her head. 'I've forgotten what that feels like.'

Matteo thought of what Fin had told him, and his heart broke for the boy and the woman doing her damnedest to make sure he'd be okay for ever.

'What you need is a holiday.'

'Chance would be a fine thing.'

'You get an allowance for leave. Use it.'

'Now isn't the best time.'

'Bet you've been saying that a lot. Don't you think it would be better for Fin *and* you if you had more quality time together?'

He knew he was skirting too close to Fin's secret, but it needed to be said.

'I work the hours I do to make sure he doesn't want for anything.'

'But money doesn't buy you happiness.'

'It keeps a roof over our heads.'

'What about changing your career, getting a job share, moving somewhere cheaper so you don't have to earn so much?'

'Wow! Opinionated much?'

'I'm sorry, I'm just—I'm trying to help.' He frowned. 'I feel like you haven't had a sounding board to bounce ideas off, and I'm offering myself up.'

Her eyes softened with her posture. 'Well recovered. And you're not wrong to say it. I know I claim to have made room for Fin in my life, but in reality, I've just crowbarred him in. I haven't wanted to give up on my dreams. The great career in the city, an amazing home with Hyde Park on my doorstep and eventually a man and a family to share it with.'

He let her words sink in, for her and for him. Because in that moment he realised they were both at a crossroads in life, unsure which route to take. Robbed of the life goals that had guided them until now.

What did one do when they outgrew their life-long dream—whether through age or circumstance?

'I think that deserves a toast.'

'A toast!' She gave a bemused laugh as she took up her glass. 'You have a very strange view of what constitutes a celebration.'

'Not celebrating, more of a promise to one another. To find a new dream, a new goal to reach for.'

She turned her head a little, eyes narrowing. 'And what if I'm not ready to give up on my old one?'

'Like me, you don't have a choice.'

She pursed her lips, a second's quiet contemplation then slowly she leaned forward.

'You know, for a man touted as being a tad vacant up there—' her brows nudged up, indicating his head '—and all about what's down there—I mean your supertalented left foot by the way.'

He laughed, his body coming alight at the fire in her gaze. She *so* didn't mean his feet!

'You're actually quite insightful.'

'I'm sure I should be feeling a little insulted at that…but does it mean we have a deal?'

'Yes, Lucky Luca. We have a deal.'

They clinked glasses, took a drink, but instead of leaning back, she stayed close, her honeyed eyes locked in his, her cheeks warm and lips wet from the wine. *Dio*, he wanted to taste them. The wine and Porsha felt like the most perfect illicit mix.

The perfect way to seal their deal too.

Especially with that look in her eye, but…

'Porsha, I—'

'Is something burning?'

They both leapt back to find Fin in the doorway rubbing his eyes and yawning wide. It took a second for Matteo to regain his senses, another to catch the same scent Fin had.

'He's right, Matteo, it—'

Cazzo. He leapt up, raced to the oven and yanked it open. 'The focaccia!'

How could he have forgotten the bread?

You really need to ask?

That night, Porsha couldn't sleep.

Weirdly frustrated and energised, she couldn't get a certain someone out of her head.

It didn't help that he was just next door either. Knowing that nothing more than a wall separated them. And it wasn't just the way he made her feel but also the way he had her brain ticking over.

In one evening, he had her pressing Pause on her life and taking time to think. To question. Was he right? Did she need to reconsider everything— the house, the prime location, her job?

She couldn't bear to fail, but was it failing if she was making a conscious choice to change it all?

'Aunt Porsha?' Her door eased open a crack, the plug-in light on the landing making a silhouette of Fin's slight frame.

'What is it, darling?'

'I can't sleep.'

She gave him a soft smile. 'You and me both.'

He lifted Ted, the bear she'd bought him when he was born, to his chin and sniffed. 'I miss Mum.'

She swallowed the lump in her throat. 'Me too.' She flicked back her quilt and patted the space beside her. 'Want a hug?'

He nodded and padded over, snuggling down beside her. She stroked the hair back from his face and kissed his head. 'Me too, kiddo. Me too.'

Because for all Sassy had been the opposite of her—wild, irresponsible and in no way dependable—she'd had a huge heart and Porsha had loved her.

'I think she would have liked Lucky.'

Porsha huffed out a breath. 'She sure would have.'

And judging by the way Matteo lived his life— the ease with which he made decisions; offering himself up as a childcare alternative without a second's hesitation; the thrill-seeking pursuits Sassy would have joined him in, the riskier the better— they'd have a whole lot more in common too.

'You like him as well, don't you, Aunt Porsha?'

More than was wise or sensible, but like a lot of things in life, you didn't always get a say in it.

She just needed to keep her wits about her and resist the other urges he stirred up, because Lucky Luca wasn't a man to fall for…he was a man to have fun with.

And that kind of fun was way off her radar.

The future needed to be secure and as stable as she could make it for Fin. That meant reducing the variable risk factors, of which a love interest on any level was most definitely one.

But a friendship…there could be no harm in that.

'Aunt Porsha?'

'Yes, darling, I think he's very nice.'

'I think he thinks you're very nice too.'

And just how nice he thought her was the question she fell asleep with…variable risk factors be damned.

CHAPTER FIVE

TWO WEEKS LATER, Matteo was in Porsha's kitchen cooking up his mother's favourite meal when his phone rang. He grinned when he saw the ID, swiped the call to answer and cradled it against his shoulder as he added extra seasoning to the pan.

'Leo, what's up?'

'What's up is that's it's Friday, and we're all heading to the club. You coming?'

He turned on the spot, grabbed another pan for pasta and set the kettle going.

'I can't tonight.'

'You have plans that beat our company?'

'Is that so hard to believe?'

'It is when you're choosing whoever it is over us. Unless…you got a new woman on the go and don't want us to know about her.'

'No, no new woman.'

'And yet you've bailed on us for the last three Fridays. What gives?'

'I'm busy.'

'Busy doing…hey, are you still looking after that kid?'

'His name's, Fin, and yeah, I'm still helping my neighbour by looking after him.'

Looking after him, cooking for them, making himself at home in her kitchen, which he'd been in more than his own of late. Letting her work the hours she needed, where she needed to do them, while he kept on top of things food- and Fin-wise. Her 'Can I think about it?' turning into an unsaid agreement as they steadily grew accustomed to having each other around. Day in, day out. Enjoying it, too.

'Helping your neighbour who just so happens to be female and available right?'

Matteo shook his head and gave a laugh. 'It's not like that.'

'She's hot though, right?'

His mind conjured her up and Matteo swallowed. 'Not why I'm doing it.'

And not what he wanted to think about either—Porsha in all her hotness.

So, why are you doing it?

Every now and then, he'd be forced to consider it, like now. Maybe she reminded him of his mother—a struggling single mum. Her parents off travelling while his mother might as well have been, for all the support they gave their only daughter.

'Come on, mate, since when have you had a female friend and not—'

'Leo!'

'Jeez, chill out! I hear you. Well, I don't, but…'

'There's nothing going on between me and Porsha. We're neighbours. Friends. Nothing more.'

And why, oh, why was he bothering to argue it out with Leo? Experience told him the guy would think what he wanted anyway, and given his track record, Matteo couldn't blame him.

No. It was more like he was on the defensive, his friend hitting on a nerve Matteo didn't want to acknowledge. Because his friend was right in more ways than one. She was hot. His body *did* want to bed her. And his head was vehemently against it. As was his heart that cared enough. He wanted to help her. Her and Fin. Not make a mess of their life and the friendship they'd all formed.

'Methinks the lady doth protest too much.'

Matteo forced a laugh. 'And methinks you need to—'

'I'm so sorry I'm late!' Porsha hurried in, soaked through from a summer downpour, wincing when she saw he was on the phone.

'Sorry,' she mouthed.

He waved. 'I've got to go, buddy.'

'Honey's home, right?' Leo teased.

Matteo rolled his eyes, eyes that caught on Porsha shrugging out of her coat, and he tried not to notice the way her white blouse clung to her. The way the sheen over her skin enhanced her natural olive glow, the pink in her flushed cheeks too. Escaped strands of hair clinging to the delicate

softness and making him want to reach out and…
and do nothing!

'None of your business, Leo.' He tugged his gaze away. 'Have a good night.'

'I'd say the same to you, but it—'

He cut the call and pocketed the phone, shaking his head. She was Fin's guardian. A friend. And *so* not his type. She really, really wasn't. Minimal make-up. Unfussy ponytail. Monochrome wardrobe…well, save for her underwear.

Cazzo! Don't go there!

'Something wrong?'

'Nope.' He went back to his cooking, stirring the sauce with extra vigour. 'How you doing?'

'Aside from being slightly damp, never better. I'm sorry I'm late though. Charles collared me as I was leaving.'

'You're fine. Take a seat, I'll get you a glass of wine.'

'I can get it. Where's Fin?'

'He's in the front room, doing his summer project for school.'

'He's doing *what*?'

He flicked her a look to find her staring at him and grinned. 'I know, wonders never cease, right?'

Shaking her head, she planted her fists on her hips, her blouse pulling taut across her front… not that he was noticing or reacting in any way, shape or form!

But *Dio mio,* he was no monk. And *this*, the

incessant pull he felt towards her, the attraction, the chemistry…

Experience told him it should have eased by now.

Instead, it was doing the opposite.

But to seek out a fling right on one's doorstep? Especially when he had no interest in commitment. Short-term, long-term—any kind of term.

And then there was Fin to consider, a boy who'd already been through enough upheaval to last a lifetime.

No, denial was the only option. Even if it was driving him crazy. Unreasonably so. More sleep, that's what he needed. Getting up extra early to hit the gym and his daily 10K before Porsha needed his services was obviously taking its toll.

Sleep? You're going to blame sleep?

'You really are a miracle worker.'

'Huh?'

Her eyes sparkled, her lips pursing to the side, their luscious pink fullness too much to bear—

Stop looking then!

'I'm worried his poor attention span is rubbing off on you though…'

He gave a tight laugh. She wouldn't joke if she knew where his head was at.

'I can't believe you've got him doing schoolwork, *actual* schoolwork…*optional* too.'

'He wanted to do it.'

'He *wanted* to?' Her eyes danced all the more. 'No bribery involved?'

He gave another laugh, willing it to sound easy when he was like a tightly coiled spring, battling the heat she so readily triggered and couldn't act on. Plus the knowledge that the bribery involved, unintentional though it was, might not reach the Porsha seal of approval.

He'd save that battle for later though, because he'd learnt one thing about Porsha…actually make that two things:

One, the woman didn't like surprises, so an ambush of any kind was never a good idea. And two, the woman got hangry. Like seriously hangry.

'So…' She came up to him, glass of wine in hand, and leaned back against the counter. 'What did you both get up to today?'

He kept his eyes on the pan. 'More football, more going out in disguise.'

'You know wearing a cap is hardly a disguise?'

'You'd be surprised how well it works, especially when you duck your head and dress unassumingly. No one batted an eyelid in the Natural History Museum today.'

She squinted up at him. 'I bet you look like you're up to no good.'

He grinned. 'No change there then.'

She gave a soft chuckle, sipped her wine. 'Maybe sticking two mischief makers together wasn't such a great idea…'

'It was the *best* idea. Besides, having Fin is like a stealth shield. No one suspects Manny Matteo to be Lucky Luca.'

'I guess they don't, but they'll work it out eventually.'

The hesitation in her voice had him glancing her way. 'I told you I won't put him at risk. If it becomes an issue, we'll change it up.'

'I know. And after all you're doing for him, how happy he is, I don't want to worry but…'

'But you do.'

It was a statement, not a question. Because that was the third thing he'd learnt about Porsha. She worried about *everything*. Who Fin saw. Where Fin went. What Fin did. Matteo understood a mother's worry, but with Porsha, it was dialled up to the max. Overanalysing every eventuality, spotting risks where there were none…

His notoriety *was* an issue, it did come with its risks, but Matteo found himself striving to find a balance between her worry and letting Fin be a child.

'Hangry?' he teased, aiming to lighten the mood.

'Always.'

She leaned over to see inside the pan, her subtle perfume rising with the steam—flowers and the rain outdoors mixed up in the garlic, tomatoes and Italian seasoning. It *shouldn't* work. He stirred faster, throwing his focus into the sauce and the lumpy whirlpool he was swiftly creating.

'It smells delicious.'

So did she.

The kettle came to a boil, and he grabbed it, eager to keep busy and save him from himself. He poured it over the awaiting pan of pasta and set the heat going.

'Thank you for doing this. All of it. Looking after him, cooking. I don't know what I would have done without you.'

'You need to stop with all the gratitude. I told you it keeps me out of trouble too.' So long as he could keep her at arm's length while doing it. 'You've given me a new purpose, and for that *I'm* grateful.'

She gave another soft chuckle, the sound working its way through him. Enticing and beguiling and *Cristo*, he needed to get food on the table so he wouldn't put her on it!

'You keep saying that,' she murmured, 'but I think it's working more in my favour, and I really wish you would let me pay you.'

'No. *Assolutamente no.* I'm having as much fun as Fin is. It's nice to enjoy football again, without the pressure and the responsibility, and that boy never tires of a good kickabout. Or indulging in an ice cream or two.'

'Just another reason to thank you. These feet are for heels and running. No more. As for the ice cream, do you know how hard it is to resist all that creamy goodness when you have it out of the freezer every day?'

He smiled. 'I do now.'

'Well, you can get away with it…'

She elbowed him in the ribs, the contact fleeting, but its effect radiated through him. He caught her eye and there it was, flashing back at him… the fire. She bit her lip and turned away.

Poor lip. What he wouldn't give to kiss it better, to kiss the bashfulness away too…

'With all that football, I meant.' She stepped away, took a breath that sounded more like a relieved sigh. 'Have you thought about making it into a regular thing?'

'Eating the ice cream or the mannying?' He laughed to clear his throat. 'I don't think so.'

She gave a smile of mock despair. 'I meant the football. The coaching.'

He shuddered. 'I have no interest in getting caught up in the pressures of the Premiership again. If I'm not playing on that pitch, I intend to keep my distance.'

Because if he couldn't be out there playing at the top, he certainly couldn't bear watching others do it from the sidelines.

'I understand that, but…' She studied him intently and he wondered if she got it. Like, truly got it. Because no one else seemed to. He was harassed daily by his ex-teammates, his old coach, manager—you name it, they pushed it. 'I meant more of an active role in the community, helping kids that need it.'

'Coaching local teams?'

'I was thinking more the creation of a centre where kids who want to play can come and learn from the best.' She beamed up at him, telling him with her eyes that he was that. No matter that he didn't feel it. She thought it. But then, she wasn't into football, didn't *watch* football unless it was him and Fin with the ball. She wasn't objective.

Doesn't mean you don't feel pumped when she says it though!

And *Dio mio*, he was blushing. Actually blushing. He *never* blushed. Unless he was caught with her bra in hand.

He cleared his throat again, stood closer to the steaming pan and hoped she'd attribute the rising colour to it rather than her.

'Just think what you could do for kids who don't have a stable home life, who need an outlet to blow off steam and keep them off the streets, out of trouble and doing something fun and worthwhile.'

'You mean kids like I was once?'

'You and kids like Fin who need a safe space and a facility that can give them what their parents and guardians can't. I couldn't have given him what you have.'

'You don't give yourself enough credit.'

'Be that as it may, there's no doubt you've been good for him.'

Matteo eyed the sauce bubbling away, inhaling its familiar scent as he mulled it over. 'A sort of therapy in disguise, so to speak?'

'Exactly. Things here have been so much…so much calmer since you came into our lives.'

'What you mean is that he's been too tired to create mischief?'

'Too happy, more like.'

And there she went again making his chest puff up.

'Which makes me even happier to have been of service.'

As for her idea, it had merit. He certainly had the money and the contacts to make such an initiative work. Not for profit and all for the good of the community. How would it feel to have multiple versions of Fin running around making progress, whether it be physically or mentally, on the pitch or in their own headspace? To be instrumental in improving the lives of so many?

A spark lit within him, an excited flicker in his gut that he hadn't felt since he'd hung up his boots. 'That's not a bad idea.'

'Of course it's not.' She passed him a glass of wine, clinked hers against his. 'It was mine.'

He took a swig, grinned. 'Humble much?'

'When it serves me to be. You have a lot to offer, you just need to see what we all see. What I see.'

And what did she see? His eyes latched onto

hers, their hazel depths captivating in their warmth, their sincerity...

He struggled to draw a breath, struggled to look away. Had someone stolen all the oxygen and dialled the heat up to the max, because it wasn't just the food that was cooking. And the colour creeping up her neck, the way her mouth parted and her eyes dilated...she was baking with him.

A *beep-beep* pierced the air. The oven. The bread. Not again!

'I'd better get that.' He spun away, took the breath his lungs so desperately needed and swapped the wine glass for oven mitts.

'Can I do anything to help?'

'It's all in hand,' he assured her, taking the tray out of the oven.

'Mmm, that looks and smells divine.' She covered her stomach as it gave a hearty growl and grimaced. 'Sorry, I missed lunch.'

Something she did far too often, he'd noticed.

'Homemade garlic bread?'

'Fin's favourite.'

'Mine too.'

He knew that as well.

And now her eyes were practically salivating over the bread, never mind her mouth, and he loved that look. Loved being able to bring it out in her. Didn't matter how tired she first appeared when she got home, how weary. His food was the magic cure and the reason he'd cooked most nights since taking on his impromptu role of manny.

And though he'd like to say it was entirely altruistic, it wasn't.

He liked having a reason to stick around on an evening. He liked catching up on her day and vice versa. He'd never thought himself lonely before, but having Fin and Porsha around felt nice.

Having people to look after nicer still.

Since losing his mother, his team had sort of filled that role, and when he'd lost his team…well, he'd lost that too.

He cleared his throat for the umpteenth time and buried the thoughts that were straying too far into the deep and meaningful…a place he rarely dared to venture even for his therapist. Because the deep and meaningful led to feelings, and feelings led to pain.

'And this dish was my mother's favourite…a classic Bolognese.'

'The true Italian way…?'

'Of course.'

'Can I get a sneaky sample?'

She looked up at him, skin still flushed, eyes bright, those escaped strands of hair just itching to be swept back…

'Of course.'

And now he sounded like a robot stuck on Repeat. He reached around her for a spoon, ignoring

the tantalising current that ran along his arm. She
was so near…it would be so easy…

He ignored it all and scooped up a small mouthful.

'Careful, it's hot.'

She leaned closer, lips parting as he offered out
the spoon. Eyes locked on his, trusting him as she
closed her mouth around the tip and cleaned it off
with a delectable hum. She closed her eyes and he
was too enraptured to move. There were so many
ways in which he could coax out similar noises,
so many pleasures they could share…

Her eyes fluttered open and he backed up
sharply.

'You like it then?'

'Am I that obvious?'

'I'm not complaining.'

No, he wasn't, but he likely should be. How was
he expected to play the platonic friend and manny
when she triggered *all* the X-rated thoughts?

'So, how did the meeting go today?' That's it,
get back to business, the boring stuff. 'Has your
extra presence in the office been worth it?'

'I hope so.' She leaned back against the counter
as he checked the pasta. 'But Charles never really
gives much away.'

'Do you think he's listened to you?'

She'd complained numerous times over that the
older man rarely did, that her being a woman was
reason enough to mute her. Though Matteo had

argued back that as Charles was the man who'd appointed her, he must see more in her than she thought.

'He asked some reasonable questions, then proceeded to ask if I had a holiday on the horizon, as HR were concerned about the number of days I'm racking up.'

'Sounds caring to me.'

'Sounds like he wants me out of the way, you mean.'

'Do you always see the bad in everything?'

She tucked in her chin. 'I'm seeing the truth.'

'You're a pessimist.'

She gave a choked laugh. 'I am not.'

'You are. Instead of seeing it as a caring gesture from your boss who is concerned that you haven't taken any time off, you see it as him wanting to get rid of you. But newsflash, Porsha, he'd simply sack you if that's what he wanted.'

'And he'd have a nasty legal battle on his hands if he did, so he doesn't dare.'

Matteo shook his head. 'It must be an awful place to live.'

'What do you mean?'

'In that head of yours.' He lightly tapped a finger to her temple. 'All that second-guessing, all that worry.'

He hadn't meant to create such a serious connection, hadn't meant to hit his mark so acutely, but watching Porsha doubt herself—whether it was with work or with Fin—he was desperate to change it. Have *her* change. Have her see herself for the woman she was. Accomplished, clever... profoundly stunning too. Not that the latter was helping him.

She wet her lips, her eyes shining back. 'And now you sound like my parents, who frankly—'

'Aunt Porsha, you're home!' Fin barrelled into her for a hug and had barely drawn breath before he looked up at Matteo. 'Have you asked her yet?'

Porsha frowned. 'Asked me what?'

Matteo sent Fin a warning look, a discreet shake of his head.

'Matteo?' She turned to him. 'Asked me what?'

'Would you like chocolate cake or treacle sponge for dessert?' he lied, though he did have both options at the ready.

'Dessert too?' She gave him a bemused grin. 'You really are spoiling us.'

'If you can't go all out on a Friday night, when can you? Besides, you deserve it after the week you've had.'

She deserved a whole lot more too. Which brought him to the question Fin wanted him to ask, but he needed to find a way in first, and that required patience.

Something a seven-year-old didn't know much about.

CHAPTER SIX

JUST LIKE EVERY meal Matteo prepared, his mother's Bolognese was utterly delicious.

As was his Italian chocolate cake. Porsha was going to have to add an extra mile to her early morning treadmill run for that delight. If not three!

She smiled across the table at the man who had made it all for them.

She meant what she'd said. Without him, she didn't know where she'd be now. What she would have done. How she would have coped.

She rarely let herself depend on anyone, but she'd come to depend on him. For her sanity. For Fin's happiness. For her daily pick-me-up.

Something quivered inside her. Fear.

Because to trust him with all of that took nerve. Nerve she wasn't so sure she possessed.

'Come on, Fin,' she said, rising from the table. 'Let's clean up while Matteo rests those talented feet of his.'

'It's okay, I'll do it,' Matteo said as Fin started to help without a grumble—another Matteo-inspired improvement. 'You need a bath, kid.'

Now Fin grumbled, '*Really*?'

'You're sure?' she said.

'*Certo.* You guys go on up.'

And there he went again, being amazing in every way.

She strengthened her smile, hoping it hid the worry because regardless of her growing feelings towards him—Fin's too—she needed to run with it for it was working.

As she went through the motions of Fin's bedtime routine—teeth, bath, bedtime story—the evidence was there in the contented child snuggled down next to her.

Barely a chapter in, his head grew heavy, his gentle snore telling her he wasn't listening any more.

She cherished the easy sound, the feel of his head against her chest, his arm locked around her middle. Loving. Trusting. *I've got you, darling.* She swore it to herself as much as him.

Closing the book, she placed it on the bedside table and eased out from under him. Trusty Ted was ready to take her place and tucking the bear into his arms, she kissed his forehead. 'Goodnight, darling.'

He stirred. 'Aunt Porsha?'

'Yes?'

His lashes fluttered open. 'Can Lucky come say goodnight too?'

She smiled softly, though deep within, the tiny flutters of panic spread.

'Of course, kiddo. I'll send him up.'

She headed downstairs to find Matteo still at the kitchen sink, pink Marigolds on, and never before had the sight of domesticity been so sexy.

Though as Matteo was swiftly proving, the man could throw himself into anything, a task as menial as housework or as skilled as football, and against her will, she'd be drawn in. But she wasn't the only one falling under his spell. She had to think of Fin. And heaven help her, she had no idea how to stop it without ruining the peace they had found.

'He's asking for you.'

Matteo jumped. Whatever he'd been thinking about, he'd been lost to it. 'He is?'

'Sorry, I didn't mean to startle you.'

He smiled wide. 'I was a million miles away.'

Which would probably be the safest place for him if Porsha was being honest with herself.

'He wants to say goodnight.'

'Oh, right, yeah, sure.' He plucked off the Marigolds and swept past her, so quick she wondered if he'd sensed her hesitation, shared it even.

She topped up their wine glasses, listening to the gentle pad of his sock-clad feet on the stairs, the quiet creak of Fin's ancient door...

She took the wine into the family room and curled up on the sofa.

It had only been a fortnight. That was all. Not long enough to form a serious attachment. And they all knew this arrangement was temporary. That Matteo was helping her out for the summer or until she could get another form of childcare sorted. Whichever came first.

Not that she had had the time to look…or the inclination.

Which was her bad.

But come winter, he *would* be many miles away. He'd already told her and Fin that he spent the season in Canada 'shredding the slopes.' To which Fin had of course begged to visit and Matteo had expertly hedged.

Though the idea of him being gone…

'He was pretty much fast asleep.' Matteo came into the room, his presence shining a ray of warmth over the chill that had consumed her, and she smiled.

She waited for him to take up his glass and settle into the sofa beside her before saying, 'I can't remember the last time I sat down to a quiet glass of wine before nine.'

'Last Friday perhaps.'

She gave a soft chuckle, sipped at the berry-rich nectar. Another from Matteo's very expensive and very rare collection. 'True, but before that—' she shook her head '—it would have been pre-Fin.'

His eyes narrowed on her, the mood intensifying with the look he sent her. 'Do you do that a lot?'

Her pulse skipped. 'What?'

'Date things pre- and post-Fin? Compare the then to the now?'

She tucked her feet under her and sunk that bit deeper into the grey sofa.

'Don't you?' she deflected. 'With your football...'

'I try not to.'

She took in his grave expression, the way he focused on the wine in his hand. 'Because you can't change it?'

'I guess. But then neither can you.'

'Difference being, I wouldn't want to. Change the fact that he's with me, I mean.' Her gut rolled with what she would change, her eyes drifting to the unlit fire that looked as cold as she suddenly felt. 'I'd change what happened to Sassy, do anything to have her back and save her. But between my parents and me, Fin is better off.'

'Because you don't want him being brought up like you and your sister were?'

She wriggled again, his accuracy unnerving her. But then she'd been honest with him from the very start. Her feelings about her upbringing and what she'd wanted from life the moment she could take control of it.

'I know it sounds awful because they always loved us, and they love Fin, but the way they brought us up, that life...it's impossible.'

'In your opinion.'

She choked on her wine, the censure in his tone unnerving her further. Or was it more that he was forcing her to question it? Her decision to push them out and protect Fin from the chaos she'd lived through.

'In mine and the majority of others who seek to have a place to call home and a settled life.'

'I had a place to call home when I was kid, a routine that you would likely deem settled, but it didn't make me happy, and I wouldn't go back to it. Not in a million years.' His voice was gruff with the memories, harsh too. 'It's the people who make you happy, Porsha, not the four walls you live within.'

She eased back, trying to imagine what it would've been like for him and realised his censure was more about his past than her vision for a future. Though she couldn't deny the question persisted: Should she be finding more of a balance? Let her parents back in. Indeed, *ask* them back in. Lean on them. Not as much or as erratically as Sassy had, but…their love and support were there to reach for. Whereas for Matteo and his late mother…

'I'm truly sorry for what you and your mother went through. That was no happy home for a child to grow up in.'

'I'm more upset for my mother, it haunted her until she died.' He huffed into his wine. 'What a hand to be dealt, eh? Pregnant at fifteen. Evicted from her village by society. Emotionally disowned by her parents. And then breast cancer takes her at forty.'

'I'm so sorry.' Porsha pushed past the sadness clamming up her throat. 'She must have been so proud of you though, to come through all that adversity and achieve all you had. You must have brought her so much joy.'

A smile played about his lips. 'It was my mission in life... From the day I brought home my first pay cheque, I aimed to spoil her. She would fuss and refuse, and I would carry on regardless. I made sure she didn't have to work a day longer than necessary, saw that she had the best care when she fell ill too...'

His voice cracked and he took a shaky breath. '*Cazzo*, see what I mean about grief? It's always there, regardless of how long it's been. Seven years and it still hurts like hell.'

She wanted to reach a hand out. Wanted to absorb some of his pain and offer him comfort. But every time they touched, she felt as though they were that bit closer to crossing the invisible line. And that line was their protection. She needed to hold it.

'But you know what losing her taught me?'

'No...'

She met his gaze, surprised by its sudden intensity, and swallowed, sensing she wasn't going to like what came next.

'She taught me life's too short. That we should

live each day like it's our last. And I don't think you're living, Porsha. I think you're going through the motions.'

She wanted to object, deny him. But…was he right?

'I think you're missing one very important element in your life.'

She frowned. 'Which is?'

'Fun.'

'*Fun*?' she scoffed.

'Yes. Fun.'

'I have fun!'

He cocked one sexy and uber-annoying brow. 'One example, *per favore*?'

'I—I…'

His other brow nudged up.

'I do fun! I—I go to Zumba on a Saturday…or at least I did pre—' She bit her lip. 'Now I join in online.'

'Online?'

'And I run.'

'Outdoors?'

'When he's at school, otherwise I hit the treadmill.'

'So, you exercise…' his eyes remained wide '…*that's* your fun?'

She wriggled her shoulders against the sofa, burying herself into its reassuring softness. 'There's nothing wrong with looking after your health.'

'No, there isn't. I'm a daily runner myself, but

there is something wrong with being a workaholic who's stretched herself too thin and doesn't take time to chill.'

And why did that sound so familiar?

'You've been talking to Fin again, haven't you?'

'He's worried about you.'

'He's a child!'

'And even he can see it's wrong.'

'He doesn't understand that adults have to work.'

'Maybe not, but he's not wrong about the downtime. When did you last go out to dinner, to the cinema, to a club? Even just a coffee shop for a catch up with a friend?'

She didn't answer.

'What about dating?'

She gulped. 'Dating?'

He gave a lazy grin. 'Yeah, you know that thing couples do for fun?'

What Lucky Luca really meant was sex. She knew it, and he was the last person on earth she wanted to touch on that hot topic with. Not when every millimetre of her body hankered after him.

'I haven't done any of that since I became a mum,' she said, her back rigid. 'My spare time is about Fin now, as it should be.'

'Only he doesn't see enough of you either.'

She paled. 'He—he said that?'

Matteo didn't answer, but she could see the truth in his face and her shoulders slumped.

'He's worried that you don't have any friends.'

'I *have* friends… I just haven't had them around or seen them much since he came to live with me. Oh God, I'm really messing up, aren't I?'

'I was going to say you've been something of a martyr…'

She shook her head. 'Because that sounds so much better.'

'Well, it beats *pitiful.*'

She knew he was trying to lift the mood while hammering his message home, and she flicked one foot out to prod him in the thigh.

'Some of us are happy with our own company and don't need a billion and one parties and a different bedmate for each one.'

His eyes flashed and he grabbed her foot before she could pull it back.

Serves you right for playing with fire, Porsha!

He squeezed on a pressure point that should be deemed a pleasure point. A thrilling shiver running through her as she bit back a moan.

'Jealous?'

He stroked his thumb up the arch of her foot and she curled her toes as the tremors multiplied.

'No,' she lied.

'I didn't think so.' Was he lying too? 'But you do need to learn to relax.'

Mentally she cursed, her mouth parting to let in air, because she was struggling to put the power into her lungs to breathe. Not when his continued caress was taking over, feeding the heat unfurling in her core.

'I'll relax when life allows me to.'

'And when will that be?'

'When Fin settles into a routine that works.' She clenched her teeth against another moan of delight. 'When work calms down and I can get my weekends back.'

'Sounds like you're waiting on the world to make it happen.'

'I guess I am.'

'You know, for a person who's spent their life taking control of it, don't you think that's a bit contradictory?'

She could do nothing but gawp, the heat given free rein as his words hit home. Because he was right. And he knew it, his smile turning smug as he stopped his mind-altering caress, but he didn't release her.

'So, how about you quit waiting, make the decision to relax and force the rest of the world to abide?'

'And how exactly might I do that?'

'By taking the holiday you're long overdue.'

'Holidays take time to plan. I need to give notice at work.'

'Notice that Charles has all but told you not to worry about.'

'I can't just pack a case and go. I have builders coming in, renovation work to oversee.'

'Not a problem. I gift you use of my property development company—project manager, construction workers, whatever you need—so long as you and Fin get away together.'

She gave a disbelieving laugh. 'You can't be serious?'

'Why not?'

'Because it's too much.'

'It isn't too much. Not to me. And the sooner your house is finished, the sooner the power tools quit, and I get my peace and quiet back next door.'

She laughed. 'Now I know you're talking rubbish, because I haven't been able to get a contractor out in weeks.'

'Guilty as charged, but you can trust my team to turn up when they say they will and get the job done properly and efficiently.'

'Well, I'm paying.'

'I wouldn't have it any other way...which brings me to my final offering.'

'Offering?'

What else could he possibly offer her? Hell, she'd already labelled him her white knight, a guardian angel...all fantastical and heavenly nonsense that she'd never put any stock in. Because her sister had, and she'd been let down spectacularly.

'I'd love it if you and Fin came away with me.'

'You want us to what?' She choked, red wine

sloshing down her white blouse as she tugged her foot from his grasp.

'That could have gone better—sorry.'

She reached for a tissue, avoiding his eyes as she dabbed at the stain and panic took over.

'You can't be serious, Matteo. If you want to go away, go. The last thing you want is to be held back by us when you could be going about your fun.'

'Don't you think it would be fun though—me, you and Fin?'

'Not the kind of fun I'm sure you'll be looking for.'

His eyes darkened, his jaw pulsed.

'That's not what I meant.' And now her cheeks were burning because she really hadn't meant what he was thinking. She meant all his thrill-seeking stunts! The hair-raising activities she had no interest going anywhere near, let alone permitting Fin to do so.

'I'll have to take your word for it.'

She'd insist and explain if she wasn't so worried it would make her look even more suspect. And weak. Her sister had called her out for it plenty of times over the years. Calling her chicken, a Negative Nelly, and she didn't want that from Matteo.

'So you're just being a pessimist again. I'm offering you a holiday, all expenses paid, and instead of jumping at the opportunity, you're weighing up the risks, losing yourself in every negative eventuality rather than grasping it with both hands.'

'I'm…'

'You're…?'

I'm scared. Scared of spending more time with you. Scared of where we'll end up—of where Fin and I will end up when you leave.

See, came Sassy's voice. *Negative Nelly.*

'Would it help if I told you Fin is very keen on the idea?'

She snapped into the present. 'You spoke to Fin about it?'

His Adam's apple bobbed. 'Not intentionally, no, I promise. He asked why he hadn't seen me around before when I live right next door. And I explained I have homes all over the world.'

'I bet you did.'

He ignored her sarcasm and continued, 'I told him I follow the seasons. He already knew about winter in Canada, but when I said I own an island in Italy with a Roman fort—'

She choked on more wine. If she kept this up, she'd be wearing more than she'd drunk.

'An *island*?'

'Yes.'

'Of course you do.' She dabbed herself down again, grateful that he'd attribute her sullenness to jealousy rather than fear. 'So, what, he asked if he could see it?'

Fin had asked to go snowboarding in Canada after all.

'*Si.*'

'And you said?'

Because Matteo had evaded the Canada one beautifully. What was different about Italy?

'I said I'd love to take him.' He had the decency to look sheepish. 'Which I now see was very wrong of me, but it just came out. In all his excitement and eagerness, and then he asked when we could go and told me how much you were desperate for a holiday and how the summer break was long and how nice it would be to do it now. Especially with the weather here taking a turn for the worse while Italy is all sunny skies and blue seas.'

He even sounded like Fin, words tumbling one after the other as he sought to convince her.

'I don't believe this.'

'I'm sorry, Porsha. It wasn't my intention to stir up trouble. But Fin is right, you do need a holiday, and I can provide you with the perfect escape, and with me there, you won't have to worry about keeping Fin happy.'

She huffed. 'Are you saying I'm incapable of making him happy?'

And that was her own insecurity talking, she knew it.

She also knew he was right. Again.

'No, of course not. But I do think it would benefit you both to spend some quality time together.'

She pondered what he was offering. It did seem like the perfect solution. Too perfect.

But then she always did see the negative in everything first. Just as he had said, just as her parents and Sassy had always said.

Maybe it *was* time to adapt. To live a little…

But to live with Matteo in his Italian home… was that wise on any level?

Who cares? Sassy would say. *The Italian stallion will make it the holiday of a lifetime!*

'Put it this way—'

'We'll do it,' she blurted, Sassy winning out.

His grin lifted to one side. 'You will?'

'I said so, didn't I?'

'So you did. And as we all know, Porsha Lang never says anything unless she's thought it through and means it.'

'Precisely.'

'In that case, I'll have my jet on standby and the island prepared for our arrival.'

'Your *jet*?'

'*Certo.* Buckle up, Porsha. You're in for some serious fun and real quality time with your nephew. I can promise you that.'

Real time with her nephew *and* Matteo…like a real family that wasn't one.

Oh, Porsha, what are you getting yourself into?

CHAPTER SEVEN

'AUNT PORSHA, Aunt Porsha, you've got to see this!'

Fin raced ahead, the same phrase on Repeat as Porsha followed at a more docile pace.

Her knees were still weak from the helicopter ride that should have been a short hop from Naples, but of course Fin had loved it so much, Matteo had insisted on taking the 'long way round,' and Porsha had taken to counting her breaths. Talking down her racing imagination that had them hitting the ground in a ball of fire while responding to everything Fin was eager to point out with the briefest glimpse and a tight smile.

And now that they were on land, she questioned whether the tragic had befallen them and she'd died and gone to heaven, because surely this was it.

She breathed in the air, its warmth divine after all the rain back home, its scent too—the hint of citrus and pine—evoking memories of long-ago summers. Happy summers when school was out and travel didn't mean falling behind. When Sassy would coax her into letting go and having fun…

Porsha's heart caught in her chest and she squinted against the sun, lowering her shades.

All around, the Tyrrhenian Sea was as blue and as dazzling as the sky above, an Elysian canvas for the golden island with its craggy cliffs and secluded coves. And everywhere she looked along the trail, trees and plants flourished, their bursts of colour and ever-changing scents a delight on the senses.

Matteo pointed out the olive groves, lemon trees, herbs and veggies...

Almost every turn in the path that led from his helipad to his home revealed a private oasis that blended into the fabric of the land. Whether it be to swim, dine or simply lounge. And at each, Fin tested it out. The water temp, the seats, the beds... she laughed as he rocked on a lounger that looked more like a piece of art than a piece of furniture.

'Isn't this place incredible, Aunt Porsha?'

'It sure is, kiddo.'

She hugged her middle, grateful her sunglasses hid much of her frown. Keeping her feet firmly on the ground was going to be harder than she'd imagined. Keeping a seven-year-old's feet rooted even more so.

She'd known it would be special. Of course she had, but nothing could have prepared her for this. If she'd needed more proof that Matteo lived in another world, she had it.

From the private airstrip in the UK to the fully

staffed private jet to the equally private helicopter and the welcome line of staff that had greeted them on arrival at his equally private island. Oh, she had it alright.

And as she'd been introduced to the team, she'd tried to act like this was all normal for her. Smiled and shook hands. More names being thrown at her than she could keep track of in her overawed state.

There was Matteo's butler, Lorenzo, the man he was currently speaking to as they followed a few steps behind. The housekeeper, Joyce, Lorenzo's wife. The gardener, Ben, who doubled as the dock hand. The cook, Chef Paolo. The pool boy, Filippo. A captain and a deck hand, Tom and Enzo, because of course there was a yacht. Something they'd spied on the way in—much to Fin's joy!

She'd known footballers were wealthy, known that Matteo was up there with the top earners. His reputation as a hugely successful property tycoon almost as big as his playboy rebel status too.

But maybe she should have googled his net worth while she was running her own version of a background check that first day, because now she just felt naive.

'If you stick to the main path, it'll take you up to the house,' Matteo called out as he paused with Lorenzo, and Fin raced ahead.

She gave him a nod, suppressing the excited leap of her pulse as she lingered a second too long on him. Like hers, his eyes were hidden behind shades, but that grin, the dimple in his right cheek, the way his dark hair had lost some of its structure in flight and begged to have a hand run through it. Her palm tingling to do the deed.

As for the sun on his bronzed skin… Matteo's Italian roots shone. The open collar to his black polo shirt revealing just enough of his chest to make her mouth dry. Beige shorts with pockets he casually had his hands in now, making them stretch across his crotch. *Gulp.* Muscular arms and legs all on show.

Heaven knew how she'd cope when he appeared in swimming trunks…

She resisted the impulse to shake off the tantalising shiver snaking its way through her, and turned back to—*Fin?*

Where in the—?

She hurried forward, spying his white T-shirt amongst the trees. *Stick* to the path Matteo had said!

'Fin, that's not the—'

'Holy smoke!' he exclaimed, coming to an abrupt halt in a clearing just ahead, but all Porsha could see was the way the ground disappeared before him, the ocean a severe drop away.

'Fin!' Heart in mouth, she came up alongside him. 'You need to be more careful!'

She placed a steady hand on his shoulder, her eyes on the potential fall…though from this angle, she could see the cliff edge was deceptive and a gentle slope started a few feet down, but still, surely there should be safety rails!

'This isn't the p—'

'What is *that*?' He thrust a finger down at the bay below, completely oblivious to her, and she followed his gaze. There, moored at a wooden pier, was the yacht they'd already seen—very modern and very sleek and very, very expensive. But that wasn't what he was pointing at. Behind it bobbed a speedboat with a giant inflatable *banana*.

'That'll be part of the water sports I mentioned.' Matteo came up behind them, still grinning, and every bit of her fizzed with his return. Until his words registered and her stomach bottomed out. 'Enzo's been testing some out with the staff this morning, they've had a blast.'

'Water sports?' She took a steadying breath. 'No one mentioned any water sports.'

'I was telling Fin what we could do here. I didn't want him thinking it would be all swimming and topping up the tan…' He gave her a wink. 'Though you're very welcome to stick to that while us boys hit the action.'

'The *action*?' She raised her brows, her voice reflecting her nerves that still hadn't recovered from Fin's swift dash to the edge.

'Hey, don't look so grey. It's all perfectly safe, I promise.'

'Safe, right.'

'Trust me.'

She swallowed. Trust him? She barely trusted herself with Fin's care, and even though she'd come to trust Matteo to look after him at home in London, where she felt she knew all the dangers and hospitals were close by, but here…here she didn't know where to begin.

'We'll see.'

'We're talking about having fun, and you sound like I'm telling you to walk the plank.'

Fin laughed. 'That's a sick idea! We can pretend you're the princess, Aunt Porsha. Matteo can be the pirate feeding you to the sharks, and I can be the prince come to rescue—no wait, hang on! I think *I* should be the pirate and Lucky can be your prince.'

She gave Fin a tight smile. 'Sounds fun…so long as the sharks are make-believe too.' She looked to Matteo for reassurance, her heart panicking once again. 'There aren't any sharks, right?'

'Sharks have more to fear from us humans than the other way around… Come on, you want to see the house?'

'You mean the fort?' Fin piped up, falling into step beside Matteo as he led the way again and Porsha hurried after them.

'Matteo, that's not an answer,' she said. 'Are there sharks?'

He dipped his chin to look at her over his sunglasses. 'If you see one, you should count yourself lucky. I've dived a thousand times around here and still haven't had the pleasure.'

'Good. I think.' Though that wasn't to say they didn't exist. Perhaps she ought to google it. Along with the safety of banana rides!

'I can't believe you own a real Roman fort,' Fin was saying. 'Wait until my mates hear about this. We must get photos, lots of photos!'

'We will,' Porsha assured him as they came to the peak of the hill that formed the base of the Roman stronghold. Standing tall and proud, its stone walls glowed warm and gold in the sun. If ever there was a building to make her think of Matteo, this was it.

'Before you go in, Fin, I have something for you.' Matteo waved to Lorenzo, who picked up a box from beside the front door—if you could call the heavy wooden structure with its cast-iron fixtures such a menial thing—and brought it over.

Matteo reached inside, plucking out a red-crested helmet, a cape and a gold sword.

'You ready to be a centurion and guard my fort?'

Fin clicked his feet together and saluted. 'Hell yeah!'

'Fin! Language!' Though she couldn't stop the smile that touched her lips, her frayed nerves easing a smidge with his Matteo-induced excitement. The man just knew how to take the extraordinary and make it ever more extraordinary. And he was such a natural with Fin. So natural she couldn't believe he didn't have kids of his own…

And really, Porsha, that's the thought you want to entertain when your feet are already threatening to float?

She shoved the thought aside, a skill she was quickly becoming good at when it came to Matteo and followed the giddy mini-Roman forward.

'Welcome to your fort, Centurion Fin, Ms Lang…'

Lorenzo bowed his head and pushed open the door into a vaulted hallway so vast and beautiful that Porsha's mouth fell open. The aged beams in the ceiling and the stunning mosaic floor spoke of times gone by, the stone that lined the arched windows and the branching corridors too.

And as each room gave way to the next, the wonder continued. Every detail so thought out and always channelling the eye to the deep-set windows with their billowy white drapes and picture-postcard views beyond. So many stairs and landings, so many bedrooms with their own unique style and adjoining bathrooms with giant oval tubs.

Until finally they reached the top…

'And this is the *pièce de résistance*, or as we say in Italy, the *cavallo di battaglia.*'

Matteo pushed open the door and Fin stepped past him with a frown. 'Cava what?'

'It means warhorse, and in this context, it means the best bit of the entire island. The watchtower. From here you can see all the way around, back to the mainland and Capri, as well as out to sea.'

'Wow! We're so high up!' Fin rushed to the edge, the height of the stone wall giving Porsha the reassurance she needed to let him be as he peered between the slits in the stone. 'And there's a pool, too—no way!'

Porsha rolled her eyes. 'I think there are loads of pools, kiddo.' She'd counted at least three big enough to do laps in and several more plunge and bubble style.

'No, there's a pool up *here*, Aunt Porsha!'

Sure enough, as she stepped closer, she could see the wall wasn't flush. It split and curved to allow access to an infinity pool, a pool that visually disappeared into the ocean far too many feet down, and Porsha's head swam. There was no way on earth she was getting in that. She rocked back to feel Matteo's hand against her lower back.

'Steady.'

The contact whipped through her and she gasped.

'Do you need to sit down?'

She gave the smallest shake of her head. What she needed was for him to remove his hand and go back down a flight or two.

'Do you get vertigo?'

'I didn't think I did. It's probably just the travel getting to me…'

And your touch and the way I'm steadily losing my head around you.

'Do you want to go and freshen up before dinner? It might make you feel better?'

She nodded and he took her hand—whether he did it consciously or on autopilot, she didn't care. She didn't trust her legs to obey her just yet.

He called Fin over and they headed back inside.

'Do I get some ice cream now? Joyce said I could have some when we got here.'

Fin was asking Matteo, but Matteo was eyeing Porsha. Concern creasing his brow.

'I think your aunt wants to freshen up first.'

'It's okay, we can do ice cream and then we'll freshen up.'

Who knew, maybe it could chill her nerves and overactive libido too.

'If you're sure then we'll—' His phone started to ring and he pulled it out of his pocket, swiped at the screen. 'Right, to the kitchen for ice cream!'

But before they'd made it two flights down, the phone rang again, and with a grimace he stalled. 'Are you two okay heading down without me? I have to take this call.'

'Of course,' she told him, letting go of his hand and immediately missing his warmth. 'You do what you need to do.'

Speak to whomever you need to.

Not that it was any of Porsha's business, but her

ears strained as he took the passage that led to his master suite, phone to his ear. 'Hey, Isabella.'

Isabella.

That was an Italian name, right? Beautiful too.

Was she a stunning local he hooked up with when here? Probably.

Porsha clenched her fists, admonishing herself. She was being unfair and out of order. Matteo could date whomever he chose. He was as much on holiday as they were. And after everything he'd done for her and Fin, the last thing she should be feeling was put out.

'Aunt Porsha.' Fin blinked up at her. 'Did you just swear?'

'No!'

'You did, you said—'

She silenced his mouth with a gentle palm. 'How about we hunt down that gelato?'

'Is that like shower gel to wash your mouth out?'

She gave a tight laugh. 'No! It's Italian for "ice cream," though it'll keep our mouths too busy for much else.'

'Sounds good to me!'

Though if soap could wash away all the unhelpful thoughts and feelings she was having, she'd devour that too…

They headed down to the kitchen to find Joyce talking to a young girl they hadn't yet met. Porsha opened her mouth to announce their presence, but they caught wind first and quickly broke away, making busy with the linen and glassware. Odd. Did they think Porsha would judge them for having a chat? Or were they talking about them? About her?

Porsha's neck prickled and she took a breath. She was just overtired and oversensitive. This whole place was a shock to the system. She schooled her features into a smile.

'Hi, Joyce, any chance we can get some of that ice cream you mentioned?'

The older woman's smile seemed genuine enough. 'Of course, Ms Lang.'

'It's Porsha, please.'

She nodded, but Porsha got the feeling Joyce wasn't about to change her polite address. As a fellow Englishwoman on foreign land, Porsha would have hoped for some rapport. Instead she felt like she was being put under a microscope. The young girl trying to discreetly suss her out beneath her lashes wasn't helping either.

'My daughter Sofia can show you what we have…can't you, Sofia?'

The young girl blushed, her long dark hair falling forward as she nodded and sought to make eye contact with Fin rather than Porsha.

'Would you like to follow me?' Sofia sent a nervous glance her way, and Porsha strengthened her smile.

'Thank you.'

With a last look Joyce's way—the woman had gone back to her cleaning—Porsha followed Fin and Sofia down to the cellar.

'Don't "hey" me, Mr De Luca. You're supposed to be in my office right now.'

'It's Matteo, Isabella. How many times do we have to go over that? And I'm sorry. It—it slipped my mind.'

'Once is believable, but twice in as many weeks…?'

Matteo shoved his bedroom door open and strode inside. 'I know. I know.'

'Then you'll also know that you've been avoiding me.'

'Avoiding therapy, more like…' he murmured, too quiet for her to hear.

Hardly the most mature reaction, Matteo. Now you sound like a disgruntled child and she's a professional, for Pete's sake. A professional with a duty to care for you. Cut her some slack. You requested her services. You pay her to do this. So deal!

'I'm sorry, Isabella, I've had a lot on my mind.'

'Are you forgetting that's the reason you came to me in the first place?'

His head travelled back to that day months ago. Sleep-deprived, a constant thrum in his veins impossible to satiate, the shakes…

'Look, Mr De Luca, if you're not willing to put

the work in to help yourself, how can you expect me to help you?'

Matteo stepped out onto his balcony and breathed in the view of the Tyrrhenian Sea and the island that had once been more than just a piece of land to him. *Should* mean more still.

'I've genuinely been busy.'

'Doing what?'

The curiosity was there, laced within her measured tone.

'I've been helping my neighbour.'

She said nothing, her silence a demand for more.

'She's sole guardian to her seven-year-old nephew and was struggling for childcare…'

More silence.

'So, I stepped in.'

'*You* stepped in?' Now her voice slipped. 'In what capacity?'

'I've been acting as her manny for the summer holidays so she can work.' He lifted his chin, proud of all he had achieved with Fin even if his therapist was likely gawking at the phone. 'I don't know what you know about seven-year-olds, but they sure keep you busy.'

'And this is out of the goodness of your heart and nothing to do with her being a single woman?'

'*Si.*'

'And our conversation about women and the role they play in your life…?'

Matteo shoulders hunched. 'For once, it's not like that.'

The line fell silent…yet again demanding more. More depth. More honesty.

'We are neighbours, friends, and I've brought them to Italy to give them an overdue holiday.'

'*Where* in Italy?'

'Where do you think?'

'You've taken them to your island off Capri?' The curiosity wasn't so much laced as it was blatant now.

'*Si.*' Heat rose within him. 'Why are you saying it like that?'

'Like what?'

Matteo spun away from the view and strode back into his room, cherishing the air-conditioned breeze against his fevered skin. 'You know, like *that*?'

'I don't know what you mean. I think you're hearing something in yourself, Mr De Luca, and maybe you should listen to it.'

He shook his head. 'You're talking in riddles, Isabella.'

She gave a soft chuckle. 'And on that note, I will leave you to your holiday, but I'd appreciate you making an appointment to see me upon your return. An appointment that you *keep* this time.'

He grumbled some response.

'And use the time wisely, Mr De Luca. You need that holiday too.'

'I feel like I've been on holiday forever.'

'Use it to reflect and retrain your body,' she continued, ignoring him. 'It takes time and effort to get over an addiction, and for you, it will be no exception.'

Addiction. How he hated that word. Hated it even more because he'd never have put himself in that box. An addict. Him.

'And I will be billing you for this session.'

Session? What session?

Though if he was honest, something within him had creaked open, made itself known... He just didn't want to examine it too closely.

'Fine. See that you do. *Ciao*, Isabella.'

He cut the call and threw his phone down on the bed, gripped the back of his neck with both hands, and stared up at the stone ceiling. The urge to take a run, hop on a Jet Ski, cliff dive, do *something* burned through him, so he closed his eyes, took a breath and another...

You don't need *it.*

Just.

Be.

CHAPTER EIGHT

'NIGHT-NIGHT, DARLING. Sweet dreams.'

Porsha bent to press a kiss to Fin's head, careful not to wake him. He'd fallen asleep before she could open his book, the day's travel and excitement finally catching up with him—her too if she was honest.

Matteo had been right to suggest feeding him earlier. If they'd kept him awake to eat with them, he'd likely have face-planted in his dinner. Something he hadn't done since he was a toddler.

And how much simpler life had been then. Erratic and as chaotic as ever with her sister and her parents at the helm. But simpler in so many ways.

It's no use looking back, came the inner voice of reason. *You can only look to the future and secure him against more of the same.*

Keeping those words close to her heart, she switched off the bedside lamp and crossed the room to her adjoining bedroom. Matteo had given them a two-bedroom suite of gargantuan proportions. With a bathroom each, sprawling sofas and reading nooks, a private bar and balcony, it was the epitome of luxury. And Porsha was way out of her comfort zone.

What did one wear to dinner when this was their life?

She slipped out of her travel clothes and entered the dressing room, surveying the shelves and rails filled with her clothing. All beautifully arranged and all without any help from her.

It was still too hot outside for trousers, so a skirt or a dress…something that suggested *I'm on holiday but I'm not out to seduce you.*

She opted for a black slip dress, knee-length. And kitten heels. Nothing too sexy about that.

Checking her appearance in the mirror, she pulled her hair back into a smooth ponytail, applied some lip gloss and a subtle sweep of blusher. There, she was ready.

If only her nerves would agree.

She left her room and headed down the multiple staircases until she hit the ground floor. Matteo had told her they'd be eating out on the terrace tonight…just the two of them beneath the stars.

Butterflies fluttered in her stomach. She and Matteo hadn't dined alone since that first night, and she'd been drawn to him then, an irresistible chemistry charged by the newness of their acquaintance.

How was she going to fare now when those feelings had only grown, evolving into something deeper, something stronger? The more she got to know him, the more she saw him with Fin too…

'Ms Lang, are you okay?'

She startled, hand on her chest as she spun to find Joyce in the kitchen doorway.

'Yes, yes, perfectly fine! Thank you, Joyce. I—I was trying to remember which side the terrace was on.'

Joyce pursed her lips as though containing a laugh. 'The terrace goes all the way around, but if you mean where you're eating, come, I'll take you.'

Porsha followed the woman outside, her embarrassment morphing into something far more potent but no less hot as she set on eyes on him.

Sat at a small candlelit table, a bottle of champagne on ice, hair freshly styled and clothes as dark as the night sky above, his eyes too as he turned to take her in.

'*Buonasera*, Porsha.' He pushed up out of his seat, and she smiled, at least she hoped it was a smile. She swore she couldn't feel her face any more for the warmth rushing her body.

What she wouldn't give to regain some of her famed corporate cool!

'Sorry I'm late.'

'No apology necessary…' he pulled out her chair '…but you best get over here before the *hanger* sets in.'

She gave an abrupt laugh as she stepped forward, careful not to touch him as she lowered herself into the seat.

He should count his lucky stars that her hunger for him didn't go the same way as food.

'Champagne?' He lifted the bottle out of the bucket, and she nodded.

'A celebration, or more promises?'

'Let's see this one as a celebration of our fresh start,' he said as he poured, the bubbles fizzing up, the sight and sound making her think of the rising sensation within her. 'We're on the road to fulfilling our promise.'

'Confident that we're getting somewhere?'

His eyes reached hers. 'When I put my mind to something, I rarely fail.'

Normally she'd agree with him. But she'd been trying for two years to figure out a new path with Fin and had failed to find it.

Then again, she was on her first holiday in that same amount of time, and Fin…well, there was no doubt he was more settled, so maybe Matteo was onto something.

She waited for him to take his seat and lifted her glass. 'To fresh starts and new dreams.'

He clinked his glass to hers, and they drank in sync, gazes hooked. The warm breeze caressed her sensitised skin as the fire in his eye caressed her from within.

She wet her lips, swallowed the bubbles that were rising back up…

'Are you ready for your first course?' came Lorenzo's voice from out of nowhere.

'Please,' Matteo said, not taking his eyes off her and she dipped her gaze, cursing the heat and her inability to control it.

'I'll let Chef know.'

'Was Fin okay?' he asked as Lorenzo walked away.

She nodded, cleared her throat before meeting his gaze again. 'He was asleep before I could read to him. You were right to suggest he eat earlier.'

He smiled and eased back in his seat. 'You know, I think I've surprised myself at this mannying.'

A laugh threatened to escape as she imagined her nephew's roll of the eye. 'Fin hates that term.'

'So do the guys at the club. They think it emasculates me, but it's no skin off my nose.'

'The club?'

'My old team.'

'You've told your friends about us—about Fin?'

She didn't know why she was so shocked. Not when it was taking up a lot of his free time. And he was good at it. Doing a far better job than she'd been able to…but for how long? At some point he had to go back to his life and then where would they be?

She touched a hand to her brow, hid behind it as she staved off the sudden chill.

'Of course. I hope you don't mind?' He frowned

across the table at her, just as perplexed by her re-action. 'They were asking why I haven't met with them recently, and I had to give them something. They're like a dog with a bone at times. Suspicious. Always quick to think I'm up to no good.'

She gave a soft chuckle. 'I can imagine.'

Lorenzo returned with their plates and Joyce hung back in the doorway. What was the woman doing? Checking they had all they needed or watching over them? Porsha didn't know, but her neck was prickling again...

'To start with, we have a caprese salad with fresh ciabatta,' Lorenzo was saying as he set the dishes down. *'Buon appetito.'*

'Grazie, Lorenzo.'

'Yes, thank you, Lorenzo.' Porsha forced her eyes to her plate. 'This looks delicious.'

And it did. Rich red tomatoes, plump mozzarella and vibrant green basil drizzled with what was sure to be home-made olive oil and a thick balsamic glaze. Golden bread that looked and smelled divine.

She just needed to dig her appetite out of the worry pit that was her stomach.

Lorenzo discreetly left, Joyce following behind, and Matteo gestured to her. 'Eat.'

But first she needed to know something. 'Were they surprised?'

'Who?'

'Your friends? When you told them what you were doing?'

He lowered his cutlery, his mouth twisting to the side as he considered his response. 'Yes. Though they put the reason down to you.'

She took another sip of bubbles, dousing the rising flutters and the heat his words had triggered.

'What you mean is, they assume you want to bed me and are using Fin to do so.'

His throat bobbed, but he didn't flinch, his eyes didn't waver from hers. *'Si.'*

The sexiest *'si'* she'd ever heard, and her laugh was choked by the lustful rush.

'I'll take that as a compliment.'

'You're not angry?'

'Why would I be angry?' Another tight laugh. 'If that was your true desire, Matteo, I think you would've made a pass at me by now, don't you?'

He didn't answer, the silence stretching, hot and strained.

'I mean, Fin's not easy to look after by any stretch of the imagination,' she hurried out, needing to say something. 'So that alone would have had you seeking your reward long before now and moving on.'

His jaw pulsed, his posture stiffening. 'Let's get one thing clear. Fin is great, Porsha. He's fun and loving, and you should be proud of him.'

'I am proud!' She cursed her choice of words, his tension seeping into her. 'That wasn't what I—'

Movement in the shadows of the house caught her eye. Joyce was back. Lorenzo too. They weren't more than silhouettes, but she sensed the woman's stare, sensed their words were about her.

'I'm sorry.' She tugged her gaze back to his, though the fine hairs on her nape and arms couldn't be so easily diverted. 'That didn't come out like I intended. I was trying to say that I thought your friends were wrong and they should give you more credit.'

And talk her body down at the same time. Remind it of the truth. That Matteo was no more interested in her than she was... No, that didn't work either. Because she *was* interested, and she didn't want to be. That path only led to heartache and disruption, none of which she wanted. For herself as much as Fin.

'*Bene.*'

Good?

Though it didn't look like he considered it good. The dark intensity of his eyes failing to free her from their grasp. He looked perturbed, unsettled by whatever he was thinking, and now she wasn't sure what was worse—Joyce and her potential mutterings or Matteo and his private thoughts.

'It is good that we're on the same page,' he said eventually. 'My friends don't know us together and cannot understand my fondness for Fin...or you. And I can't blame them, because if someone had told me a month ago that this is what

I'd spend my summer doing, I wouldn't have believed it either.'

She was still dizzy over the 'fondness' remark. Matteo was fond of her, of them. She knew he was fond of Fin—that was obvious enough. But her?

'We're fond of you too,' she admitted, her body warming, her heart too, as she gave up trying to control it. 'And grateful.'

He gave a small smile, the tension around his eyes easing. 'Now eat. Chef's caprese salad is more than just a salad, his homemade balsamic takes it to another level.'

She nodded, watched as he tucked in and went to do the same, but another twitch in the shadows drew her up short. Still watching. Still talking. She understood staff being at your beck and call, but this…

'What's wrong?' Matteo asked, gesturing to her plate. 'Is it the dish? Because—'

'No, no, I'm sure it's fine. I'm just—I'm being silly.'

'In the time I've known you, not once would I classify you as being "silly", so out with it, Porsha.'

She lowered her lashes and took a breath. 'I don't think Joyce likes me.'

'*What?*' He went to turn and she kicked him underneath the table, regretting the contact almost as swiftly. How could he fire her up when she was *this* on edge?

'Sorry.' He leaned closer, whispering with her. 'I don't understand.'

'She's talking about me to Lorenzo, I'm sure of it. And she was doing the same with her daughter earlier. Clamming up as soon as I came into the kitchen…and the curious looks she keeps giving me.'

'Ah…' His eyes lifted and he leaned back in his seat.

'What do you mean "Ah"?' His unexpected ease had her feeling the exact opposite.

He took up his drink for a long, extended sip.

'Matteo! If you don't explain it to me this minute, I'm going to storm over there and demand she tell me herself.'

'You don't want to do that.'

'No, what I want is for Fin to relax while we're here, and even though he's a child, he'll pick up on it quick enough, and then he'll be the one making a deal of it. And we all know where that'll end up.'

'More bra trebuchets with Joyce as the unassuming target?'

'You mean, catapults.'

'Not the way he was using it.'

'He showed you—No! Don't tell me!'

'I can draw you a diagram if you like…'

His eyes sparkled in the candlelight, and Porsha prayed he'd attribute her glow to the flame too, or a day in the sun, anything but him talking about her lingerie.

'Quit it and tell me what's going on!'

She gave him another prod with her foot, and this time he countered the move, hooking his own around her ankle and trapping her there with his other.

'Easy, tiger.'

'Don't you "tiger" me.'

Their gazes were locked and loaded, the connection beneath the table as strong as the one blazing above it.

'They're simply wondering.'

'Wondering *what* exactly?'

'What it is about you that makes you special.'

She blinked, her pulse stalling. 'Sp-special?'

'*Si.*' His eyes raked over her face as though coming to some realisation himself. A realisation that he wasn't quick enough to share, and her pulse started to race again.

She took a breath. 'In what sense?'

He held her gaze a second more, everything about him so very still, and then he cleared his throat, and his eyes drifted to the horizon. To the land in the distance and its flurry of tiny lights, the odd twinkling boat too. But as stunning as it was, the only view Porsha was interested in was the view inside his head.

She leaned forward, easing her foot from his slackened grip. 'Matt—'

'I've only ever brought one other woman here, and that was my mother.'

Her eyes widened with a breathy, 'Oh.'

'And here I am bringing you, a woman and her boy, to stay, and I imagine they think there is a lot more to it.'

'More…like your friends do?'

'No.' His mouth twitched. 'Not like my friends at all.'

And what was that supposed to mean?

His eyes returned to her, but they'd lost their ease of moments before. He looked…troubled. 'I would take their curiosity as a compliment, Porsha.'

A compliment? She pondered the magnitude of what he was saying. To be the only woman in…

'How long have you owned the island?'

He shifted in his seat. 'A while. I bought it when the building was a ruin, and my mother still had her health. It was meant to be my greatest gift to her, a safe space for her to return to her roots whenever she so desired…'

'She missed Italy?'

His smile twisted. 'My grandparents made sure of it. They brought their traditions with them, insisting we spoke Italian in the home, always regaling her of the things they loved, the things they missed, too.'

'Is that why you still come out with Italian now—your grandparents insisting you speak it?'

'And punishing me when I spoke English. Yes.'

She shook her head, sad for his mother, distraught for him, *horrified* by them. Unable to understand. 'Why would they do that?'

'To make her pay. To make me pay. Hell, I don't know. I gave up questioning their reasoning a long time ago. Long before they were gone.'

Resentment vibrated in every word, and she knew it stemmed more from his love for his mother than his hatred for them.

'And so you bought her an island…' Her heart ached and warmed in one.

'There can be no judgement on a private island, only beauty and tranquillity and everything I wanted to give her. She was diagnosed the same year, gone the next. She never saw it like this.'

'Oh, Matteo!'

Her stomach hit the floor with his unguarded pain, and she reached across the table and covered his hand with hers. She didn't care that Joyce likely watched on and would read whatever she wanted into the gesture. She only cared for him.

'I'm so sorry. I wish life didn't have to be so cruel.'

He gave her a wistful smile. 'At least she got to see it. Even if it was only once.'

She stroked her thumb over his hand, her desire to comfort him overriding all else. 'What did she make of it?'

'I told her my vision for the place, my vision being what you see today…' He gave a choked laugh. 'You know what she said?'

'No…'

'She said there was one thing missing.'

'And what was that?'

Because Porsha couldn't think of one. This place had everything…even a chapel from the sixteenth century and home-grown food aplenty.

'A family to fill it.'

Porsha gave a soft huff, feeling a sense of affinity with the woman she had never met as their dreams aligned—a home, a family. 'I think I would have liked your mum.'

'She would have liked you too.'

Her heart melted, her every urge telling her this connection was special, this was more…

'So—' she wet her lips, tried to focus on the conversation not the confusing, dangerous ramble within '—what did you tell her?'

'That she was my family and it was for her.'

Porsha smiled. Of course he had. 'And that placated her?'

He dragged a breath in through his nose. 'My mother knew me better than anyone…it didn't stop her pushing her dreams on me whenever the opportunity arose.'

It wasn't really an answer. Or maybe it was. Maybe he knew it hadn't placated her but didn't want to say so.

'Parents like to think they know best. It doesn't mean they're always right.'

'Agreed.'

He took a sip of his drink, eyed the rising bubbles in the glass before saying, 'My mother was never happy on her own. She spent her life seeking someone to fill that void, always on the lookout for love and never finding it.'

Her brows drew together as she thought of his mother's pain, knowing that the woman died alone worrying that her son would suffer the same fate. 'That's so sad.'

'It is. It's why I refuse to do the same. Life's too short to keep searching for something that doesn't exist, and you can't miss it if you're not looking for it, right?'

For the briefest moment, Porsha had believed they were on the same wavelength. That he refused to die alone too. And the tiniest hope had soared with it...

Only to be dashed when he then confirmed the opposite. And worse, he was looking to her for an ally, someone to wholeheartedly agree with his bleak outlook on love.

'Are you saying you don't believe love exists?'

'I'm saying I believe in certain kinds of love. The kind one has for a parent or their child or a close friend. But the whole instalove, destined-to-be-together-until-your-dying-breath kind of love... it's the stuff of legend. A myth. I think people are fooling themselves in the long term. Once the lustful fire dies, what you're left with are the ashes that drift away on the wind. Nothing.'

His analogy was poetic but chilling. 'You really think that?'

'I do.'

She fought the urge to retract her hand as telltale goosebumps prickled along her arm.

'If you're lucky, no one gets hurt,' he continued. 'Unlucky and one of you gets burned, the scar staying with you. Never healing. Festering and destroying what heart you have left to give.'

'Is that what you think happened to your mother? That her love for your father broke her for anyone else?'

'She was too young.'

'Doesn't mean she didn't love him.'

A grave nod. 'No and when I was younger, she told me stories of him. Of how strong and good he was. How he would have loved me given a chance. If our families hadn't intervened.'

'Why didn't she ever find him again? When you were older? When she had control of her life again?'

'I asked her that once. She told me she tracked him down, found he'd married. Had children, *many* children. He was happy, and she didn't want to destroy that. Though in truth I think it destroyed her more, seeing him so happy and settled with another. The other woman having the life that should have been hers.'

'But what about you? Surely you deserved to have the chance to know him?'

'He never knew I existed. Our families made sure of that. His family were wealthy, influential...'

'So, you know who they are? Who he is?'

He nodded.

'And still you haven't reached out?'

'The past is the past. If he wanted to reach out, he could have. He could have found her like she did him. No. He made his decision to move on, and so have I.'

Porsha studied Matteo quietly, recognising the pain of rejection in him, and questioning his decision. Surely what he needed was closure and to hear it from the man who was his father regardless. Fin had no choice but to live his life without knowing. Matteo, on the other hand...

'Do you honestly think you're that done with it? With him?'

Matteo pulled his hand from beneath hers and Porsha suppressed a shiver, curling her fingers into her palm.

'A few years after we left, my father's family fell on hard times. They lost the stature they valued above all else and were cast out by the community. To my mind, that's closure enough.'

'You mean payback?'

'Karma,' he said, his mouth a grim line, eyes hard.

She shuddered anew. She'd never seen him like this. So cold and unrelenting.

'So, in answer to your question, Porsha, I have no desire for that kind of love in my life, not when it has the power to do more harm than good.'

'I don't know,' she said softly, bravely. 'My parents, for all their faults, still love one another, they make their—' she wrinkled her nose, not wanting to think about it but saying it all the same '—continued passion for one another quite evident.'

He gave a cool smile and raised his glass in salute. 'Well, good for them. There's always a rare exception to the rule…'

She returned his smile, but she knew it lacked the same enthusiasm.

Could he really be so cut off from love? And if he was, how did that fit with all the women he'd been reported dating, and what about this Isabella? Not that she knew anything about the woman and her relationship to Matteo. Porsha was the one jumping to conclusions there, but…

'Was everything okay with your call earlier?'

Subtle, Porsha. Very subtle.

'My call?'

'Yes.' She hid behind her champagne. Took a steadying sip. 'Isabella, was it?'

Could you be any more obvious?

The waves crashed rhythmically against the shore, the cicadas chirruped, but Matteo said nothing.

'I'm sorry,' she said when she couldn't take it any longer. 'I didn't mean to pry…'

Yes, you did.

'Isabella is my therapist. I was supposed to have a session today.'

Porsha's mouth parted. *Say something, anything!*

But what could she say?

Porsha hadn't thought she could feel any worse. Turned out she was wrong.

CHAPTER NINE

MATTEO KNEW PORSHA was stewing. Knew she'd put two and two together and made five where Isabella was concerned.

And he should be rescuing her, but he was stewing too.

He stared back at her. The light of the candle accentuating her luscious mouth that had fallen open, her overbright eyes that were laden with guilt.

'I'm sorry I mentioned it,' she whispered.

'That makes two of us.'

Too cruel, Matteo. It's not her fault you acted like an arse, wasting Isabella's invaluable time. It's not her fault you're unsettled by the attention of Joyce, your therapist and your friends, every one of them making a huge deal of your actions and drawing their own conclusions.

And it's not their fault either, he realised.

Because now that he was here with Porsha, confiding in her, he could understand them all and take a wild guess that Isabella's reasoning for his motives sat somewhere in between Joyce and his friends.

In between love and sex.

He could readily balk at both extremities, but that grey area in the middle, where both passion and feelings exist, he was hovering right there. And it wasn't a safe place to be.

Not when it had him like this—on edge, downright uncomfortable in his own home—and he was taking it out on Porsha. The last woman on earth he wanted to hurt.

'Sorry. That wasn't fair of me.'

'No, it was,' she hurried out. 'It was me who overstepped. Forget I mentioned it and let's eat.'

She smiled as she took up her cutlery, but it didn't warm her eyes, didn't warm him like a smile from her usually would. And she wouldn't look at him now either as she focused on the dish she hadn't been interested in touching not two minutes ago.

He owed her something. She'd trusted him with Fin, opened up about her own worries, and he'd given her snippets in return. Snippets that could see her walking away to protect herself and Fin from the mess he represented. And he wouldn't blame her.

'You didn't overstep, Porsha. It struck a nerve, that's all, and I took it out on you. It's my own guilt.'

Her eyes widened a little. 'Guilt?'

'My therapist is highly regarded in the field. She has a long waiting list and a busy schedule. To miss one session is bad enough, but the session today was to replace one that I missed a fortnight ago when I took Fin to meet the team and—'

'You should have said! Fin could have gone any time, and I would have coped…'

'I didn't *want* to do it another time.'

He hadn't wanted to go at all, because he hadn't wanted to tell Isabella about Porsha or Fin and have questions asked that he didn't want to answer. The kind of questions he was having to face now courtesy of everyone around him and his own actions.

'So you were avoiding it? Using me and Fin to…'

'Yes.' He couldn't bear the way the truth landed.

'Why?'

'Why the avoidance or why the therapy?'

She hitched a shoulder. 'Both.'

'The former must be obvious…' He swallowed down the discomfort. 'I'm a man who doesn't do weakness in any shape or form, and there's nothing quite like therapy to make one crumble.'

'Didn't you once tell me, we all have a right to be human?'

He laughed softly—*she's got you there*.

'That was different.'

'How? Because I'm a woman.'

'No.'

'Then explain it to me…'

Explain it? His eyes drifted to the inky black horizon, to the sight of the moon rippling along the surface of the water, appreciating its serenity for all the turbulence within.

'If you'd spent a minute in my old world you'd understand. The slightest hint you're not quite with it, and the bench becomes your best friend. It's how I lived for so long…'

'But that's not your life any more.'

'No. It's not.' And it was killing him. 'Hence the therapy.'

'I see.'

He forced his gaze back to her. 'Do you?'

She nodded, the bob to her throat suggesting she struggled to swallow, her eyes damp at the corners.

'I also think it takes strength to admit you need help, Matteo. To do something that opens you up so entirely, breaks you down so that you can piece yourself back together stronger and happier than before.'

He lifted his glass to his lips and took a sip as her words eased apart the twisted mess within, letting in light, some relief—he shook his head. 'For a woman who's going through so much herself, you have the remarkable power to make a lot of sense where there has been none.'

She gave a small smile. 'And yet I've never had the courage to do what you have and face it all.'

He held her gaze. 'Who says I've faced any of it?'

'You're trying, you're in therapy, *trying*. That's more than I can say for myself.'

'And do you need therapy, Porsha?'

'Some would say I do.'

'And what do you say?'

She gave a small shrug. 'I say that right now, my priority is Fin and his happiness. Mine can come later.'

'And do you not think his happiness is intrinsically tied to yours?'

She blinked back at him. 'I've never thought of it like that.'

The urge to make her happy, her and Fin, increased tenfold.

'Which makes this holiday even more important for you both. You need to relax and enjoy yourself, spend real quality time with him. No work, just fun. May your every wish be my command...'

Something about her smile gave him pause. 'What?'

'Nothing.'

'That look in your eyes begs to differ.'

'I just had a vision of you shirtless, dressed in harem pants, appearing out of the neck of a bottle...'

He gave a hearty chuckle, the heavy mood lifting with it.

'I'm sorry to disappoint you, Porsha, but rubbing my lamp will end in a very different way, I assure you.'

And where in the hell did that come from?

Colour bloomed in her cheeks, her eyes dancing all the more as he cursed his wayward tongue. Seemed the playboy in him wasn't so far from the surface after all.

'Is anything wrong with the starter, Signor De Luca?' Joyce appeared out of the ether, and judging by her ruddy cheeks, she'd caught his blasted comment.

'No, Joyce, it's delicious, I'm sure. Porsha and I were—'

'We were getting carried away with the conversation,' Porsha filled in for him when he fell short and Joyce gave Porsha a knowing smile.

'In that case, I will leave you both to it.'

'See, she does like you,' Matteo said as the other woman hurried away, using Joyce's interruption to wind the conversation back to its initial spark.

'I'm going to have to take your word for it.'

She took up her cutlery but made no attempt to eat. And this time he knew it was down to him and not their audience.

'I'm sorry,' he said quietly. 'I shouldn't have said that. It seems—it seems that when I'm around you, I don't think before I speak. Like that first day I met you, I told you what it had taken months for Isabella to coax out of me. *Hell*, I told you

I had a therapist! Something most of my oldest friends don't know. But I was less forthcoming with my reasons, and that was wrong…especially after you'd left Fin with me.'

'When you put it like that, as Fin's guardian I should have asked *all* the questions, but if I'm honest…'

She toyed with the base of her flute.

'If you're honest?' he pressed when she failed to go on.

She lifted her gaze to his, her brow furrowed, eyes puzzled. 'For some unknown reason, I just… I trusted you.'

And why did that simple statement make him feel like the king of the world? A king who took a sudden dive when she added, 'Or maybe in my desperation, I didn't want to question you?'

She paled anew, picking up her drink and taking an overzealous swig. 'Oh God, I'm an awful parent!'

'You are not!' He forgot his own distress in the face of hers, reaching out to touch her hand still resting on the table. 'How can you say that?'

'Because I should have been putting his safety first, not the situation I was in or the joy on his face.'

'And don't you think his joy was the true reason you went along with it? Don't you think you *were* putting him first?'

She searched his gaze. 'Without any references, any checks, nothing.'

'Save for the thousands, if not millions of statements online regarding my integrity. I may be a renowned playboy—' her fingers twitched, warm and soft beneath his own '—but no one would dare question my integrity or trustworthiness. And no one could tell you anything that would give you doubt where Fin is concerned, Porsha. I'll protect that boy with my life, don't doubt it for a second.'

'That's just it, I don't.'

Her words fired through him. The bond between them deepening, precious and unrelenting, and heading somewhere he didn't understand. Didn't *want* to understand.

'As for my therapist…she's helping me with everything you already know or suspect. She's helping me find my feet after football, to find a new way living, a new purpose…'

'Like our deal?'

'Like our deal.'

'And is it helping?'

He huffed and smiled softly. 'I don't know, I guess you could call me a work in progress.'

She returned his smile. 'If football was your life for over two decades, it will take time to find yourself without it.'

'It's the addiction that's hard to kick.' It came out raw. Raw with his forced acceptance. Raw with the confession he didn't want to make but owed it to her.

'Addiction?' Her nose wrinkled. 'To football?'

'To adrenaline. According to my therapist, I'm what's known as an adrenaline junkie.'

'And do you think she's right?'

'I know I can't go a day without burning up a sweat, hitting the gym or the trails,' he chose to say. 'I know I'm always looking for the next big challenge, and if I'm honest, those challenges tend to come with a safety warning of some kind. But when you've lived your life under contract, forced to abide by the clause that prohibits such activities, it stands to reason you go looking for it once the chains have been lifted. And I know I struggled to find peace without experiencing the intense buzz that has always come before it.'

She wet her lips, her eyes flickering. 'Sounds kind of dangerous.'

'I know. And it's the reason I went to see Isabella. Many junkies seek their fix in drugs and alcohol and end up six feet under. I wouldn't be the first ex-sports personality to go that way. I chose to chase adrenaline and almost ended up the same way.'

'How?'

'I was free-soloing when I lost my grip...' He shook off the fear that gripped him with the memory.

'Free-soloing?'

'Rock climbing without rope.'

She looked green. 'Why would *anyone* do that?'

'For the buzz.'

'I didn't read about that when...' Her cheeks flushed.

'When you did your due diligence for Fin?'

'I'm not sure I'd call it that, but yes, when I checked you out. In the online sense, not the...' She waved a hand at him without looking. 'Not the physical.'

'Physical?' He cocked a brow. He shouldn't tease her, but he couldn't help it. He liked Porsha's coyness. Wrapped up in her confidence. It was refreshing and appealing, and he liked it more than he should...

'You know what I mean!' She rolled her eyes at him, sipped her drink. 'So are you still...free-soloing?'

'No. Funnily enough, it's lost its appeal.'

'And what are you trying instead?'

He laughed and she raised her brows.

'If I told you what my therapist wants me to try, you'd laugh, too.'

'Try me.'

'Mindfulness.'

She pressed a hand to her lips as she almost spat her drink, her eyes sparkling. 'You're right, I just don't see it.'

'In my defence, I was trying the day your bra came over the fence...'

Her smile along with her blush was everything.

'I swear that bra comes up far too often.'

'It certainly gave me the adrenaline rush mindfulness lacked.'

She gave a pitched laugh. 'Not what your therapist had in mind.'

'No…she believes I need to actively seek peace instead of my next high.'

'And what do you think?'

'I think, aside from my daily run and gym sesh, I haven't needed the other pursuits since you came into my life. I'd call that progress.'

Progress? Or have you simply found a new addiction?

His pulse tripped over itself, his gut twisting. Was that what Porsha was to him? Her and Fin. Some new way to get a buzz from living?

He could hear Isabella in his head as he thought it, could feel her censure across the miles…

'Now let's eat,' he forced out, calling a much-needed end to it all. 'This isn't going to get cold, but I'd warrant our main dish is.'

CHAPTER TEN

TRUE TO HIS WORD, Matteo ran every morning. Porsha suspected he also hit the gym before that too.

And he wasn't the only creature of habit.

Four days in and she'd taken to starting each day with a swim in the pool, timed such that she would be relaxing on a sun bed as he appeared on the track that wove its way up to the pool terrace. To her.

And though her head was always in a book, her eyes behind her shades were always on him.

Half-naked, every bronzed and well-honed muscle glistening in the glow of the rising sun…the man could go into advertising if he so desired. Men and women alike would queue up for a fraction of what he was offering, and she was no exception.

There was a part of her—a very small, very quiet part—that admonished her ogling, but she couldn't help herself.

It was the one time during the day when Fin was still asleep and the only sound in the world was the wildlife and the equally wild beat of her heart.

And this morning, he returned to her on cue.

'*Buongiorno.*' She lifted her sunglasses to meet his gaze as he slowed his pace to a walk. Too much skin on show. Too much for her ovaries, which were all too willing to dance in his presence. 'Good run?'

'Always.' He swept his hair back from his face, every exposed muscle in his upper body flexing up-close. *Oh my.* 'Good swim?'

'Very,' she murmured, returning his easy smile. Something she was getting well versed in doing, regardless of her racing thoughts and pulse. 'This place is too beautiful. You know that, right?'

What she meant was, *You're too beautiful!*

He grinned, a lock of dark hair falling across one eye and lending him a foppish charm that had her belly doing somersaults.

'There's no such thing as too beautiful, *cara.*'

Cara—what did that mean? It sounded sweet. Unguarded, too. Was that what a run did to him? *For* him?

She made a note to google *cara* later and watched him take a slug from his sports bottle, his eyes narrowing as they returned to her.

'Can I ask you something?'

'Sure.' So long as it wasn't, *Why are you drooling?*

'Don't take this the wrong way, I'm curious is all…'

'And you know what curiosity did to the cat…' she teased over the trepidation.

'I'll risk it with the nine lives and all.' His grin tilted, the dimple in his cheek deepening. 'Do you ever wear colour?'

'Do I *what*?'

She looked down at her black one-piece, her insides squirming under his attention.

'I mean, I know your underwear comes in other colours…'

The boyish grin made a return…as did her stomach-saults!

'But your outerwear…it's all grey, black, white…'

She pushed herself up to sitting. 'I *wear* colour.'

'When?'

'When I feel like it.'

'And why don't you feel like it now? You're on holiday, relaxing in the sun. You could carry off so many colours with your forgiving skin tone and those eyes… You were made for colour, Porsha, but it's like you choose to blend into the background.'

His open appreciation had the illicit heat rising, along with her hackles.

'I don't choose to…' She broke off at his raised brows. How was this man so astute? So attuned to her and her quirks? Not even her closest friends had bemoaned her wardrobe choices. Her sister and her parents, yes. But everyone else…

He hit the outdoor shower behind her, rinsing away the sweaty sheen and her mouth salivated anew…even with the ongoing censure.

'If you met my family you'd understand.'

'How so?'

Porsha wriggled her red-tipped toes. *See, colour!* As for the rest of her…she knew the reason well enough.

'Growing up, my family always stood out. My parents, my sister… And I don't mean in a good way,' she stressed. 'It was as though it was their mission in life to look at current trends and wear the total opposite. The more vibrant and garish the better.'

'Nonconformists. I like it.'

She scoffed. 'Easy to say when you didn't have to suffer because of it. Every event, every public outing, I would die a thousand deaths. A trip to the shops, to the park, and don't get me started on parents' evening—' she shuddered '—those that they managed to attend at any rate. Most of my peers feared what the teachers would say, I feared what my parents would wear, and *then* say.'

He stepped out of the shower, dried off his face. 'You know what I think?'

She pressed her lips together. 'I'm not sure I do, but you're going tell me anyway.'

'I think you have a wild side trapped within you and you fear letting it out. Yes, you've conditioned yourself to dress like you do, and in the boardroom, I'd wager it works in your favour…'

Her favour? What was that supposed to mean?

'…but it's a crying shame, Porsha. Because you

could rock every colour of the rainbow and people *would* look…for all the right reasons.'

And with that, he left, his observation lingering on the warm citrus air. Dizzying. Electrifying. And everything in between.

Matteo didn't break his stride until he was in his private shower, the jets on high, temperature on ice.

And still his body heated over.

Normally he'd stay and hold down a conversation—a *proper* conversation—before leaving to get ready for breakfast.

This morning, however, he couldn't stand it. Not with his libido hitting an all-time high and no Fin to prevent him from saying or doing something foolish.

He was getting far too accustomed to Porsha being there, mostly naked, deliciously bronzed, always hot AF.

He knew he sped up his 10K run so that he could get back and see her lying there on the same sunbed, same book in hand…

And acknowledging the reason for his pace, coupled with its reward in the flesh, had sent his body into overdrive. He'd hit the freezing outdoor shower in the hope it would help. But his body had mocked him. His eyes too, as they'd been far too eager to drink her in. And then he'd gone and practically told her.

Though in reality, Porsha could wear any colour and he'd be just as enraptured. Because the more he was around her, the harder it became to remind himself of all the reasons they couldn't cross that line.

Because crossing that line would bring with it an inevitable finality he didn't want to face. And the thought of no longer having Porsha and Fin in his life saw him through the remainder of his shower and back outside. Body refreshed, his mind less so.

'But you said that yesterday—' Fin was tugging on Porsha's arm as she sat on the edge of her sunbed '—and the day before and the day before that and...'

'I couldn't have said it the day before that because we just got here, kiddo.'

'Hey, hey, what's all this?'

'Lucky!' Fin came running up to him, rugby-tackling his legs in a surprising show of affection that left him winded.

He patted his back, caught Porsha's eye over the boy's head and gave a smile. Hers was tepid in return. Tepid because of Fin's nagging, or him?

Likely him. He'd overstepped. He never should have questioned her wardrobe choices. It was wrong. Thoughtless. And he'd tell her as much as soon as they were alone again.

'Aunt Porsha says no banana again.'

'No banana?'

Porsha stiffened and realisation dawned. 'Ah, you mean the ride.'

'Yes, the ride!' Fin rolled his eyes. 'What *other* banana is there?'

The one you eat, but he didn't think either of them was in the mood to hear the obvious.

'The sea is perfect for it today, Porsha,' he assured her, aware that she was going to take some coaxing. 'It's quite calm out there.'

She turned and looked out over the water. Gentle breaks of white in an otherwise sea of blue. Had she thought he was lying?

'*Please*, Aunt Porsha. I wanna have some fun.'

'And we are having fun, right here,' she said, her smile weak, brow furrowed. 'Or so I thought.'

'We were. But I'm bored of swimming races in the pool and sand forts. I wanna go in the sea. I wanna ride the banana and go on the boat.'

Matteo sympathised. To be this close to the ocean and not to have dipped a toe in…

He hadn't questioned it before now, figuring both Fin and Porsha preferred the pool to the sea. Now he wondered how much of it was down to Porsha and her own aversion.

'What do you say, Porsha? I can take him if…'

Eyes wide and unflinching met his. 'How often have you gone out on the banana?'

He cocked a brow. 'Personally?'

She nodded.

'This particular banana, not at all.'

Her nose flared. 'You can't vouch for its safety…?'

So that's what she was worried about? The safety of a contraption thousands, if not millions, used daily at beach resorts the world over?

'But I've been on many just like it in the past, and they're great fun. In the right hands, they're perfectly safe. And Tom and Enzo are nothing but careful.'

She chewed her lip, still weighing it up, still worrying about what could go wrong…he shouldn't be surprised. This was Porsha, after all.

'Everyone wears a life jacket and a helmet. Tom will stop the boat the second anyone comes off—not that anyone will come off,' he hurried to add when the colour in her cheeks continued to fade. 'But if they do, Enzo will alert Tom and they'll be straight on it. My team knows what they're doing, I promise.'

'Please, Aunt Porsha, please pretty please pretty please…' Fin went back to tugging on her arm. 'Bobby says they went on a donut when she was in Ibiza at Easter, and a banana is so much cooler than that!'

She gave a shaky laugh. *'Okay. Okay.'*

Fin froze, eyes bugging out. 'Okay?'

She nodded and he pumped his fist. 'Yes!'

'You're sure?' Matteo said and Fin's eyes shot to his, silently screaming, *Don't question it, dummy!* But Porsha's smile was too tentative for Matteo's conscience to bear.

'I'm here for fun, right?'

Though it didn't sound like she thought of it as fun.

It sounded like her worst nightmare.

'It really is fun, Porsha,' he assured her. 'Cross my heart and hope to—' wrong words, wrong words, her face was as grey as the floor '—pie!'

'Pie?' Two sets of eyes stared up at him, mouths pursed around their laughter.

'It's an Italian thing,' he lied, far too relieved to see the lift in Porsha's demeanour to care. 'And if we're doing this, we best go now and save our appetite for later. Don't want breakfast making a return.'

'*Ew*, no!'

'Now?' Porsha said over Fin.

'Yup, last one to the beach is a rotten egg…'

He spun on his heel and chased after an already racing Fin as Porsha got to her feet.

'Hey!' she cried. 'Unfair advantage!'

'All's fair in love and war,' Matteo threw over his shoulder, taking great delight in the colour now back in her cheeks and the playful spirit in the air.

Until he registered the L-word in the witty comeback, his sanity sparking as her eyes met his…

Way to go in keeping it fun and light, Matteo.

Porsha wasn't walking on air, she was running on it.

How Matteo succeeded in taking her from a

sea of despair to cloud nine in a heartbeat was beyond her understanding, but she was rolling with it, almost tumbling in the sand as they reached the cove…

Right up until she reached the water's edge and her eyes settled on the contraptions floating between the yacht and the speedboat. Vessels she hadn't seen before or expected to see now.

She froze as the sickness quelled within her, frightful images rising up that she didn't want to see…

'Winner!' Fin declared, both fists in the air as he reached the wooden walkway where Enzo was busy coiling rope.

'Champion,' Matteo declared, lifting Fin by the waist and giving him a victory swing.

Porsha looked on. Knew Fin was giggling, that Matteo was grinning, but all she could do was shake her head. Their noise died down, but her head still rolled with her gut, her eyes back on the sea and the danger it represented.

This was a bad idea. Stupid. Foolish. Just because Matteo claimed she didn't 'do' fun, didn't 'do' colour! He might as well have labelled her chicken while he was at it for all she'd responded to the playground tactic.

She sucked air in through her nose, swallowed the rising bile.

'Hey, Porsha, you coming?'

She didn't move, couldn't speak, welcomed the

sting of her nails as they bit into her palms. Matteo lowered Fin to the ground and the boy rushed towards her, Matteo setting a more cautious pace behind.

The sea washed over her feet and she curled her toes into the disappearing sand.

'Aunt Porsha—'

'Sorry, kiddo, I was wrong. I don't want to do this. Come on.'

She offered out her hand as he came to an abrupt halt, eyes wide, wearing his disappointment like a shroud. 'But, Aunt Porsha, it's going to be fun. Like *real* fun!'

She shook her head, the sickness continuing to rise as her imagination ran wild—scenes, images, what-ifs…

'Are you okay?' Matteo asked, taking hold of her arms, his worried gaze searching hers.

'No,' she whispered.

'Hey, Fin—' he looked over his shoulder '—go and see Enzo a second, he needs to fit you for a life jacket.'

'He doesn't need one if we're—' she began, but Fin had already run off, happy to follow Matteo's instruction over hers.

'I don't want him going out there either,' she said through gritted teeth. Fighting the sadness, the fear, the tears that wanted to rise, and her anger now too.

'What is it?'

She swore her knees were about to give way, that she'd crumble to the floor without his continued hold.

'Porsha?'

'I just—I don't want to do this.'

'You were fine a moment ago.'

'I wasn't fine. I wanted to make Fin happy. I didn't want to ruin his fun. I didn't want you to think I was no fun. No colour. No fun. Remember.'

She couldn't look him in the eye any more and wrapping her arms around her swimsuit-covered middle she eyed the swash. Favoured its steady regularity.

'And what changed?'

She didn't respond, not immediately. She was too busy processing his question. What *did* change?

Her gaze drifted back to the wooden walkway, to the docked yacht, the speedboat and its bright banana, to the two small yet lethal heaps of metal bobbing in between. She gulped down the sickness, goosebumps breaking out as she shivered in spite of the sun.

Matteo followed her gaze, frowned. 'The Jet Skis?'

She said nothing. *Couldn't* say anything.

'Porsha?' His eyes returned to her, their depths as soft as his voice.

'Yes.'

It came out so quiet she was surprised he heard

it, surprised even more when he said, 'What happened to Sassy?'

How could he…? Was he inside her head? 'How could you know?'

Her teeth started to chatter, and he muttered something in Italian, pulling her into his arms.

'You're saying a lot without saying a lot.'

He said it into her hair, the brush of his lips, a warming caress against the chill. She sagged into him, needing more. More heat, more strength. Took all the comfort he was offering and summoned up the truth.

'She was on one when it happened…' She squeezed her eyes shut. Swallowed. The images she didn't want to see, coming thick and fast. It had taken months to stop the accident playing over and over in her head—*not* that she'd seen it. But she'd read the reports, been told enough. 'She was backpacking in Bali. Always on the lookout for something crazy and wild to do. She never thought about the risks, she just…' Pain stole her voice, her breath. 'She lost control. Came off and hit her head. The thing had—she couldn't—she wasn't—'

Stop! You've said enough!

She buried her head into his chest, willing the imagery away, willing the cold away too.

'Oh, *cara*.' He hugged her tight, pressed his lips to her hair. 'You should have told me.'

She was still shaking. Still reliving. 'They're dangerous. It's all dangerous.'

'It was an accident, Porsha, a *freak* accident.'

She shoved him away, glared up at him. 'An accident that wouldn't have happened if she'd been more careful…people like her—like *you*—you take risks! Unnecessary risks! And when it catches up with you, we're the ones who pay the price.'

He greyed before her eyes, but she couldn't take it back. She wouldn't, because it was true. He was like her sister in so many ways and he made her feel every emotion, just like her sister had too. Knowing which buttons to press. Forever making her feel. And it was terrifying.

'Fin!' she called out. 'Here. Now. We're going back to the house!'

'But, Aunt Porsha, I've got my jacket…look!'

She couldn't look. She didn't want Fin to see her like this, but neither did she want to leave him here with those *things*. With Matteo too.

She was angry. So angry.

And in that moment, he was the target of that anger whether it was just or not.

CHAPTER ELEVEN

MATTEO WATCHED THEM GO. The disappointed slump
to Fin's shoulders and the fierce hunch to Porsha's,
a war of posture and emotion. How had it gone so
wrong?

Stupid question.

He raked a hand through his hair, blew a breath
out over the ocean.

Because there was his answer staring back at
him. He'd brought her right up against the pain of
her past, her fears coming to the fore.

He'd been so pleased to change her mind. To
see her choose fun over worry. Overjoyed, too, in
Fin's delight. He hadn't stopped to think about a
possible connection.

And now, it all made sense.

So much sense he was angry with himself for
not uncovering it all sooner. Before making such
a huge and painful mistake.

When he joined them on the terrace, Fin was
slumped in a lounger, Porsha on her haunches beside him talking too soft for Matteo to hear.

'Signor De Luca?'

He turned to find Joyce in the open doorway, fresh towels in her arms.

'I wasn't expecting to see you all back from the beach so soon.'

'Me neither.' He walked up to her, his eyes drifting back to the solemn pair beside the pool. 'Would you mind taking Fin for some ice cream?'

'Ice cream? But it's break—' she broke off, awareness dawning. 'Oh, right, yes, of course. Ice cream and pancakes, the breakfast of champions.'

Smiling wide, she called out, 'Master Fin! Sofia's clearing space in the freezer, do you fancy helping her by gobbling up some ice cream? I have pancakes, too.'

They watched as a subdued Fin eyed his aunt, and at her small nod, he rolled off the lounger, a hint of sunshine creeping back in. 'Is there a chocolate one?'

Joyce grinned. 'Of course! Best hurry though, as that's Sofia's favourite too…'

Fin legged it inside, Joyce taking a steadier pace behind.

'Thank you, Joyce,' he called after her.

'My pleasure.' Her eyes flitted to Porsha. 'You look after that one. She's lovely, Matteo, truly lovely.'

It wasn't often Joyce dropped the formal *Signor*, but when she did, he knew it was with affection.

He waited until the patio doors were closed before turning to find Porsha sitting at the pool edge, eyes downcast as she swirled her legs in the water.

'Hey…' he came up beside her '…mind if I sit?'

'It's your pool,' she said, lifting her gaze to the horizon rather than him. Though he imagined what she was seeing was the past. Torturing herself with it. Angry with it.

He sat down, close enough he could catch her sun cream on the faint breeze, feel the warmth of her bare skin, and he fought the urge to wrap her in his arms again. Worried he'd spook her when all he wanted was to have her open up. To ease her burden by sharing it with him.

'Have you talked to anyone about what happened?'

'No. Like I told you before, I haven't the courage you have.'

'You have the courage, *cara,* believe me.'

Her legs stilled in the water, her knuckles flashing white as she gripped the pool wall. 'I don't want to think about it, let alone talk about it.'

'But you're bottling it up, and one day it's going to ravage you from the inside out. Take it from someone who knows…' He watched her closely with his words, ready to back off at any moment. 'I'm no professional, but that eruption on the beach is only a glimmer of what you have going on inside of you. It's not healthy, and I think deep down you know that.'

'I think deep down I'm angry, *so* angry with her.'

'You blame her for what happened?'

'She was irresponsible. She didn't weigh up the risks beforehand and see sense. She just did it. Just like she always did. And she never put Fin first. *Ever.*'

'She was young, she couldn't have been more than—'

'She was eighteen when she had him. Not as young as your mother, and not once have I heard you accuse her of the same.'

No, that was true. But then maybe if his mother had put herself first, she wouldn't have lived such a measured and lonely existence.

'Though the truth is…' She bowed her head, took a small breath. 'I blame myself more.'

'*How*? How can you possibly blame yourself?'

'Because I should have talked some sense into her long ago. I should have called my parents up on indulging her all the time. I should have woken her up to her responsibilities and seen to it that she changed.'

'You really think that would have worked, that you could have changed her?'

'Yes. No. I don't know.'

She angled her face away, but he caught the way her bottom lip quivered, could hear the tears in her voice. 'All I know is that I should have tried.'

'Ultimately, the only person with the power to change her was herself. Not you, not your parents and not Fin.'

She said nothing. Did nothing. Had she even heard him?

'We're all unique in this world, *cara*. Some of us crave stability, others crave the freedom to live each day as it comes. Neither is wrong. It's a personal choice. But what happened to your sister was a freak accident. You couldn't control it, and neither could she.'

'She could have avoided it though,' she whispered. 'Had she weighed up the risks first and saw sense. She could have.'

'Weighing up the risks wouldn't have changed anything for her. It's no more dangerous than riding a motorbike, and billions of people do that every day.'

'I don't like those either.'

No, he didn't suppose she would.

'But I bet you see no issue with riding a bicycle, yet far more people are injured on one of those every year…'

'There's a lot more people riding them.'

And why on earth was he pointing out more dangers when he was supposed to be making her see that there's a healthy balance to be found. Between living life in fear and dicing with death. Neither extreme was healthy. He should know.

'It could have happened to anyone, Porsha.'

'But it happened to her…' she choked out, crumbling into him and he wrapped his arm around her shoulders, held her as he kissed her hair.

'I loved her, Matteo. She was annoying and frustrating and selfish, but I loved her, and I miss her every day.'

'I know, *tesoro*, I know.'

Silence fell over them, the warmth of the ever-rising sun failing to sink beneath their skin.

'But you can't live your life in fear. Scared that the same fate will befall you, that you will leave Fin without a mother figure…'

She lifted her head. 'I'm not.'

He held her gaze, waiting for her to see the truth, and when she didn't say any more, he pressed on. 'You see the negative in everything first. You imagine the worst possible eventuality and focus on that.'

Her eyes flickered, but she didn't refute it.

'Yes, your sister may have taken more risks in life than you, she may have pushed things too far at times for fun, but at least she was having it.'

'Are you seriously bringing up my lack of fun again?'

'I'm talking about the fact you spend so much time weighing up the what-ifs that you're not actually experiencing life, the thrill of it.'

'You can keep your kind of thrill, thank you very much.'

He chuckled softly. 'I'm not asking you to free solo, but a bit of harnessed rock climbing wouldn't hurt.'

She shuddered. 'I've decided I do have vertigo.'

'Do you, or are you thinking about what would happen if you fell?'

'Aren't they one and the same?'

'No. One's a medical condition and the other's your mental health. A very different beast. You get lost in your own head. In the hundred and one different scenarios, all of varying degrees of horror, that your brain presents you with. And I'd say you had acrophobia, but with you it's a fear of anything you can't control, not just heights.'

'Wow, I thought you were trying to make me feel better.'

'I am.'

'By pointing out all my flaws?'

Her eyes were wide, their wounded depths drawing him in...there was so much he wanted to say, so much he wanted to do.

'We all have flaws, Porsha, that's what makes us human. But if we let those flaws take over, we let them define us, and with you... There is so much in life to experience—that you *deserve* to experience—and I fear you never will.'

And in that moment, *his* deepest flaw rolled into *his* deepest fear, because he wanted to kiss her. He wasn't concerned with the risk of crossing that line, he wanted it gone, but his greatest fear was hurting her. Her and Fin.

Which brought him to his next point...

'And it's not just you who will suffer, but Fin too. He's a child, Porsha, you need to let him be one. You need to let him have fun, experience new things, exciting things.'

'I want to but…' Her words trailed away, her worries taking over.

'Like any kid, he'll need guidance,' Matteo reasoned. 'There'll be things he wants to do that he shouldn't, and you need to be able to advise him. With rational thought. Not fear.'

'And what if I call it wrong and he gets hurt?'

'The benefit of making mistakes is that we get to learn from them. But we have to be allowed to make them in the first place…or else we end up stifled, frustrated. When I think about how he was when I first met him, all that frenzied pent-up energy… You can't keep him caged his entire childhood.'

'No, but I'd like to wrap him up in cotton wool. Or bubble wrap. I'm not fussy,' she tried to tease.

'And you'll end up creating a monster,' he teased back. 'One who wants to do everything and anything all at once the first chance he gets. So desperate to experience the world that he won't think about the risks at all.'

She trapped her bottom lip in her teeth.

'Or perhaps worse, he'll end up like you, experiencing none of it.'

She gave a soft huff. 'You say that but the one time I let my guard down is the only time I've ended up in A & E.'

'Really?'

'I was fourteen…' She looked away as he lost her to the memory. 'My parents had some friends visiting and asked me to take the kids to the park. It was only across the road, and I was the responsible one, so they didn't question putting the kids in my care.'

'What happened?'

Her eyes flitted to his. 'My little sister got under my skin. She was berating me for being boring, telling me I didn't know what fun was…'

He sensed her pain as his conscience pricked him, guilt for telling her the same.

'They'd had this army slide put in—one that you grip with your hands and launch yourself off. Well, Sassy was all over it, everyone was…'

'Everyone except for you?'

She nodded. 'She had them all teasing me, calling me names… Anyway, I did it. Panicked. Lost my grip. Broke my arm. Lesson learnt.'

'And you've paid the price for it ever since… though your arm healed long ago.'

She raised her elbow, rotated her wrist as if making sure.

'You're right, I know you're right,' she said eventually. And he knew she wasn't talking about her arm even though that's where her focus remained. 'But it's hard. That was a moment in a life that was in a constant state of flux. I was desperate to control what I couldn't. Desperate for stability, a sense of normality.'

'What is normal?' He shrugged. 'Damned if I know.'

'But it's not this…'

'No. There's a balance, Porsha, and you need to find it. Just like you need to let your parents back in more. As much for Fin's sake as your own. They're your support network, but more importantly, they're your family. And they won't be around forever.'

She cast him a speculative look, her mouth parting but nothing coming out.

'What is it?'

'I—it's just…when you say that, it makes me think of you and your situation. Your mother gone but your father—' She bit her lip as he jerked back. 'I'm sorry. I just—you have another family out there, with a dad and the means to find him but—'

'I have no father.' The very idea chilled him to the bone. 'Just because he was involved in my conception, it doesn't make him a dad.'

'But what if there's more to what happened? What if—'

'Nothing can excuse his absence all these years, Porsha. *Nothing.*' He pushed away the long-buried questions trying to surface, the age-old wound too. 'Now quit deflecting and agree to live in the now a little more. Stop worrying so much about the future and let a little excitement in. Try new things.'

'Like riding a banana?' she suggested, waving the white flag. The emotion still there but an encouraging playfulness too.

He chuckled softly, glad he hadn't pushed her away with his brutal honesty or his own deflection.

'It would be a start. I reckon, according to statistics, it'll be safer than crossing a road in London any day of the week.'

'Now *that* I can believe.' She laughed, rubbing up against him and firing up his skin. The acute pang of desire as painful as the past he wanted to forget. 'But maybe not today, eh?'

'Why not?' He beat back the heat to focus on what truly mattered. Porsha and fun. *Platonic* fun! 'What's the saying? "Don't put off until tomorrow what you can do today"?'

'I prefer the saying "You should quit while you're ahead."'

He grinned. 'Then tomorrow it is!'

Wide eyes blinked up at him, dazzling in their intensity, twinkling with their humour. 'You don't give up, do you?'

'When it's something I want…' He held her gaze, a thousand wants rising within him, but the one he wanted most of all was the one he couldn't permit. 'Never.'

CHAPTER TWELVE

YOU NEED TO let him have fun, experience new things, exciting things...live in the now... You need to—

'This is so cool!'

Fin's exclamation broke through Porsha's mental mantra. Matteo's advice that she'd had on Repeat ever since they'd stepped into the water.

Now they were on the bobbing banana. The great big inflatable between her legs. Fin's far too wriggly, overzealous form in front of her. Matteo's far too invigorating presence behind her. And she wished she'd delayed it by another day—another year even!

'"Cool" isn't the word I would use...' she muttered as they were towed out to sea.

'Stop being a Negative Nelly, Aunt Porsha. It's gonna be a blast.'

Her grip tightened. 'What did you call me?'

Fin gave her a smile over his shoulder. 'Mum used to say it... She'd say she loved you but wished you weren't such a Negative Nelly all the time.'

'Eyes ahead!' she instructed, concern for his safety overriding the nerve he'd unintentionally poked.

Negative Nelly...cheers for that, sis!

'Hey...' Matteo leaned forward, so close she could feel his hot breath on her shoulder. 'You okay?'

She gave a hurried nod. 'Why is it I can command a boardroom full of difficult execs, but put me on an inflatable banana and my knees turn to jelly?'

'You'll be fine,' he promised. 'I've got you.'

And, oh, how you wish that was so...in every sense of the word.

She pushed the unhelpful thought aside, a thought that sounded an awful lot like her little sister's goading.

'And if he falls off...?'

'I'll be right behind him fishing him out.'

She nodded.

'Think of it like a roller coaster on water...'

'Are you *serious*?' She wanted to gawp at him but didn't dare turn around.

'You never know, you might even enjoy it.'

She gave a tremulous laugh. 'Don't bank on it.'

'You ready, boss?' Enzo called out from the speedboat.

Matteo leaned closer, his proximity an invigorating caress along her already sensitised spine. 'Do you trust me?'

She licked her lips.

'It's a simple question, Porsha.'

Only it wasn't, because if she was honest, she

felt a lot more than trust towards this man. 'Do you *trust* me?'

'Yes!'

Because she did. He was wild and rebellious, he conformed to his own rules, like her parents, like Sassy, but she trusted him. Whether it was wise to or not.

He gave Enzo a wave. 'Go for it!'

And the rest was drowned out by her squeal…

Matteo may have ridden his fair share of banana boats in his youth—it was the reason he'd had one shipped in for Fin—but he'd never enjoyed it as much as this.

And although he'd done it for Fin, he knew most of his thrill came down to Porsha.

Witnessing the change in her. Seeing her go from squealing in fear to whooping in delight with Fin. Her grip never eased on the handle. Her body never left its braced position against the spray. But as Tom threw them around, *she* was the one signalling to Enzo that Tom could go faster. She was the one telling them to hit the waves created, dialling up Fin's enjoyment too, and Matteo revelled in the whole darn lot.

When they finally returned to the beach, bodies blissfully battered by the waves, it was Matteo who'd called it a day. Not Porsha. And certainly not Fin.

'So?' he said to her as they shucked their helmets and life jackets, handing them to a waiting Enzo.

'So…' She beamed up at him, and he wanted to bottle that look. Show it to her every time she doubted something in her future. Remind her of the buzz it gave her to live in the moment and let fun in.

'Hated it.'

He drew back. 'You didn't?'

'Of course not, silly.' She rolled her eyes and poked him the ribs, her jest as surprising as the contact, and he wanted to reach out and grab her retracted hand, tug her in and kiss her deep. 'It was great.'

He forked his hair instead. 'You scared me for a second.'

'Can we go again tomorrow?' Fin begged, hopping from one foot to the other. 'And the day after and the day after that?'

Porsha frowned down at him. 'Do you need the toilet, Fin?'

'Nope. Just more fun! 'Specially now that Negative Nelly is gone.'

'I'll give you *Negative Nelly*…'

She started tickling him, his giggles rolling with her laughter, and Matteo's heart felt fit to burst. A sensation he'd never felt before. It was weird, disconcerting, but it flowed through his veins as readily as oxygen.

'Hey, boss!' Enzo poked his head out of the beach hut where he was stowing everything away.

'Joyce has just called down. Dinner isn't far off if you want to go freshen up. She figured Fin would be ready to eat a horse by now.'

'A horse?' Fin wrinkled up his nose. 'I ain't eating a horse.'

'It's a saying, silly.' Porsha ruffled his hair. 'It just means you're hungry, right, Matteo?'

'Eating *cavallo*…?' He shrugged, enjoying the playful tease which was far easier to deal with than the seriousness of where his head and heart had been travelling. 'When in Rome…'

'But we're *not*, right?'

He thought about teasing her further, but Fin's cheeks were rapidly losing all colour. 'No, not today.'

'Not *any* day,' the boy declared. 'And I'm going to make sure Aunt Joyce knows it.'

He ran off and Porsha gave a tired laugh. 'I better go and rescue Joyce.'

'It's okay,' Enzo said, jogging ahead. 'Take your time, I'll keep an eye on him. I need to take these empties up for Joyce anyway.'

They watched him go and Matteo swallowed. This wasn't good. No company. No buffer. Just them.

His blood had been racing enough before…his mind too.

'Are you tired?' he said, thinking of the way she'd sounded when she'd laughed.

She turned to face him. Her simple black one-piece looking anything but simple against her curves. The wild sea-crisped hair. The flush to her cheeks. But it was her eyes and that smile that got to him most. Wide and dazzling. So vibrant, so very…

'I feel alive, Matteo!' she gushed, arms outstretched as she took the words right out of his mouth. 'More alive than I've felt in years!'

His heart soared, desire too quick to follow. He struggled to draw a deep enough breath, struggled to say aloud, 'And you look it.'

He curled his fingers into his palms. 'You look…beautiful.'

She stilled, the slightest crease forming between her brows. 'Matteo?'

'We should go.'

He hoped by saying it aloud, his body would obey. That she would obey. Instead, she stepped closer, curious eyes searching his…

'Matteo?'

'We should go,' he repeated helplessly.

'You keep saying that.'

'And yet you keep coming closer.'

She tilted her head, licked her bottom lip and he clenched his gut against the rush of heat.

'Because your eyes are telling me something else.'

'Ignore my eyes, Porsha.'

She reached up, fingers soft as they combed his

hair back from his face. 'I don't want to ignore your eyes.'

He clamped his jaw shut. Desperate for her to stop. Desperate for her race ahead too.

'They're the windows to your soul. They're a part of you. And right now, they're telling me something I can't ignore.'

Her hands curved around his neck, and slowly… *so very slowly*…she eased herself up his body, lightly brushing her front against his naked chest. And he couldn't breathe, couldn't move, couldn't risk…

'What are you doing, Porsha?'

She blinked up at him. 'What it seems you won't…'

'What are you doing, Porsha?'

Her head, the teeniest part that was still functioning, repeated his cautionary question back at her.

Yes, what are you doing, Porsha!

This, she mentally declared. *I'm answering the need firing in his eyes, in my core.*

She was done being all serious and considerate. Boring and unsurprising.

She swept her bottom lip against his parted mouth, catching his upper lip and dragging it with hers. Prolonging the contact, drawing it out…because she wanted to give him the opportunity to stop her or because she wanted to savour the contact, she couldn't say.

Only that the heat liquefying her limbs had her clinging to him through necessity as much as need.

He groaned low in his throat. 'We shouldn't do this.'

'I'm done being sensible and responsible and safe,' she said, putting her thoughts out there for him to understand. 'You've made me feel again. And I want this.'

He shook his head, his nose brushing against hers, his lips too. 'You don't know what you're saying, you're still high on the fun. Your blood is firing with adrenaline, clouding your judgement...'

'My judgement is working just fine. You know I never speak without thinking first, and believe me, I've thought about this enough.' She lowered her gaze to his mouth, voice husky with all her imaginings. 'I want to take your advice and live in the now, embrace the fun and forget the what-ifs.'

'But this is different, Porsha. You know that.' His breath melded with hers, every word a tease. 'Sex makes things messy, complicated...and I don't want to ruin what we have.'

'Now who's talking about the risks and the future instead of living in the now?'

She closed her eyes and nipped his lip, wanting to punish him for going back on his word. To taste and tease him too. He bit out a curse and her eyes flew open. Struck by the heat and hardness in his, she fell back.

She'd gone too far, she'd pushed too—

And then she was off her feet, crushed to his chest as he swept her back across the sand.

The beach hut surrounded them on all sides as his mouth came down on hers, fierce, unrelenting. He forced her lips apart and pleasure tore through her, the salacious ache between her legs deepening with every thrust of his tongue. *God*, this was everything.

She raked her hands down his back, savouring the muscles that bunched and flexed. Hooked her legs around his waist and felt his need straining against her, obliterating any scrap of doubt that he wanted her just as much.

He set her down on some hard surface, swept an arm out to clear it of obstacles, and things hit the deck, but she had no idea what. Everything was about him and her and this. This explosive need that had been contained for weeks and finally set free.

Forking a hand through her hair, he tugged her head back. Dragged kisses from her lips to her jaw, nuzzled her hair as he whispered against her ear…

'*Dio*, you taste as good as you look.'

She moaned some nonsensical response, tightening her legs around him as he dipped to her throat.

'Temptation as rich as any chocolate,' he brushed against her skin. 'Impossible to resist.'

Like gasoline on an already flaming fire, his words combusted within her.

'Then take me.'

He lifted his head to meet her gaze, held it as he hooked his fingers beneath the strap of her swimsuit. And as he eased it down her arm, his gaze followed, his eyes firing as her aching breast spilled free. Her nipple prickled against the air, a second's exposure before his hot mouth descended.

She cried out as he sucked the puckered nub inside. Whimpered as he rolled it with his tongue. Bit her lip as he grazed it with his teeth.

His eyes returned to hers, watching her as she watched him. She wasn't sure what turned her on more—the fire in his gaze or the skill of his tongue, teeth, mouth...

He tugged the other strap down and she arched back, planting her hands into the surface behind her. Offering herself up to him like a feast, uncaring of how wanton, how desperate she looked...

He tossed her swimsuit aside and straightened, his heated gaze sweeping over her. His murmured *'Sei bellissima'* as hungry as the look in his eye. Never had she felt so beautiful, so desired...

'Tesoro.' It choked out of him as he rocked against her, his clothed hardness catching her sweet spot and she all but lost it. Her cry almost pained.

'Please, Matteo, no more teasing.'

She hooked her hands into his shorts, and he caught her wrists with a curse. His voice as raw as her throat felt.

He couldn't mean to stop. Not now.

'What is it?' She blew her hair out of her face, confused, frustrated. 'Is someone coming?'

'No.' He ducked his head like he couldn't bear to look at her and panic welled with her disappointment.

'Matteo?'

'I have no protection.'

Oh God. Surprise morphed into shame. How could she have been so stupid? So foolish? So, *unlike* herself. *Too* unlike herself. It was one thing to throw caution to the wind, but this…

Matteo was right. Again. She wasn't thinking clearly at all.

But before she could say any more, he was dropping to his knees.

'What are you—why are you—'

He tugged her hips forward to meet his lips, and she had his answer in the heat of his mouth upon her, the flick of his tongue.

'*Oh my God*!'

Her hands flew to his hair as heaven and hell consumed her. Pure heat and illicit thrill. His growl of satisfaction working through her. She'd never…had never…

He hooked her legs over his shoulders, held her steady to his delicious ministrations and she quit thinking. Only felt. The ocean rolling beyond the open doors nothing on the intense waves rolling through her.

She fell back against the wood, clawed the rough surface as he effortlessly took her to the brink, rocking and wailing like a woman possessed.

And maybe she was.

By him.

'Matteo!' she cried as the mighty wave took her. Her orgasm pulsating through every limb as her entire body thrashed with such pleasure. The likes of which she had never known with another. Not ever.

He stayed between her legs, gently caressing, supping, soothing until the waves ebbed and she could gather a breath. Gather her thoughts enough to say, 'Wow.'

He gave a lazy chuckle. Rose up her front. Kisses and tongue travelling all the way until he reached her mouth, his eyes meeting hers, dark with unsated lust.

'Wow back at you.'

He dipped to pick up her swimsuit, eased it over her legs as he stepped between them once more.

'But what about you…?'

His erection pulsed against her. 'Dinner is coming.'

'I'd rather you were…'

He swallowed her statement with his kiss. A kiss that delved deep and triggered too much for such a short duration. 'Later.'

Porsha, true to her word, hadn't thought about anything beyond the now. But she couldn't deny the way her spirits soared at the word 'later.'

He helped her down off the ledge and led her back outside. The gentle breeze teased her sensitised skin, her nipples like pebbles. But they had nothing on Matteo and the straining evidence of his need.

She stifled a giggle and he spied her focus.

'Keep that up and I'll make sure you suffer for it…'

'Is that a threat or a promise?'

His eyes flashed. 'What would you like it to be?'

'A promise. Definitely a promise.'

He shook his head, his eyes alight. 'I fear I've unleashed the animal in you, Porsha Lang.'

'Too late to cage me now.'

And it *was* too late. Because for all it had been crazy, wild, irresponsible even, would she do it again?

In a heartbeat.

And she *would* do it again, because he'd promised her. And Matteo was a man who always kept his promises.

Just as she always kept her word.

CHAPTER THIRTEEN

AN AIR RAID siren was going off in Matteo's head as they left the beach hut, warning of imminent danger.

So many scenarios playing out that ended in hurt. Fin's. Porsha's. His. Because hurting them *would* hurt him. There was no doubt about that.

But was he overthinking it?

If Porsha was okay, the one woman who considered every action to the nth degree…

But as she'd told him, she wasn't thinking about the future any more. She was doing as he'd requested, reaching for the fun. However short-lived.

And short-lived it would be, because it always was with him. It had to be.

He wouldn't travel the road his mum had, seeking the impossible. Love in all its imagined sweet perfection. And he wouldn't be his father, taking the heart of a woman and leaving it irrevocably broken in his wake.

So, what was this? A short fling. A secret fling at that. Because they couldn't risk it getting out, couldn't risk Fin learning of it and confusing it for more…

Now it's you *writing what-ifs about the future.* You *worrying instead of living in the now.*

He released her hand, careful to create distance now they were back out in the open and would soon be in company. Marvelled at the way the contact still tingled in his palm and raked it through his hair, turned but didn't let his eyes reach her. The path was long but not long enough for the lingering evidence of their tryst to calm if she were to ignite it again.

And one look at her would surely do that.

'You okay?' he said.

'Of course…'

Though there was a tremor in her voice—fear, confusion, emerging worry now the lustful haze had lifted? And it served as a timely damper on his need, making him pause at the pool terrace and meet her eye. 'Are you sure?'

'So long as you are…?'

She frowned up at him and he wanted to reach out, stroke her hair behind her ear and kiss it away.

'I don't think I can look at you without thinking of you letting go…whether it's on the banana or in the beach hut.'

She lowered her lashes, her cheeks blushing. 'Today's been something of a—'

'Lucky! Aunt Porsha! Look!'

Fin was racing across the terrace, a remote in his hand. 'Enzo said I can use it!'

Then he heard it, the unmistakable buzz of a low-flying drone. Sure enough, the thing appeared over the trees beside them, and he bit back a groan.

Just what they needed. Fin with a bird's-eye view!

Grazie a Dio, he hadn't been given it earlier... in time to catch a mindless Matteo backing his aunt into the beach hut!

Porsha gave a tight laugh, clearly entertaining the same thought. 'That's pretty cool.'

'It sure is, kid. Now I'm going to hit the shower before dinner.'

'We'll do the same,' Porsha said.

And now all he could think of was her naked under the jets, and the heat was quick to fire, the tension too...

He upped his pace, needing the space to clear his head and his body. Made it to the sanctity of his room with only a passing wave in a hovering Joyce's direction... Joyce and her curiosity that he'd likely piqued with his strung-out display.

He hit the shower. But no amount of space or cold water could cure him of the buzz. The frenetic thrum to his veins that thrived in her presence and persistently nagged when not, craving to return. Eager to hear her laugh, see her smile, make her want, make her his...

Just like an addiction.

Isabella clawed her way in, cautioning him, labelling it as some kind of fix…

Porsha, *a fix.*

'Cazzo!' He swore up at the jets, pressed his palms into the solid tiles above his head.

What are you doing, Matteo? What are you allowing to happen? What are you risking? Don't be a fool. A selfish, hormone-driven fool. She isn't the kind of woman you mess around with and move on. This isn't who you are.

Only, Porsha got to him. Got to him like no other woman had before, and he had no learned response to that. No way of knowing where the Off switch was.

But he needed to find it. And quick.

Because heaven help him, above all else, he *wasn't* his blasted father.

But what if there's more to what happened?

That's what Porsha had said. What if "more" was something like this? What if his father had felt this way about his mother? Was there more to understand?

He growled up at the jets, at himself, trying to stop the agonising onslaught. Because what did it matter? Why question it after all these years?

Because she's making *you question it. She's testing* your *limits, making you feel so much while picking apart your past and forcing you to face it.*

Was it any wonder he didn't know where his head was at?

Grinding his teeth, he slammed the shower off and got ready in a haze. Throwing on a dark shirt and light trousers, he glared at his reflection in the mirror. On the outside he was ready, but inside…

He returned to the terrace where the table was laid out with a buffet-style spread, though he wasn't really seeing it. Lost in the buzz thrumming hard and fast through his veins, filling up his head. And the second Porsha joined him, stunning in black silk, he wanted to march her back inside, to his room and his own undoing. Because ravishing her was the least painful and most blissful of all the future scenarios clouding up his mind.

And maybe once he'd done that, he'd be able to think straight again!

'Gah.' He winced as his jaw protested.

'Something wrong?' Joyce asked, placing down a tray of *spiedini*, her wise eyes far too aware.

'It's all delicious,' Porsha said for him. Was *everyone* aware that his head wasn't at the table? 'But so much food, I don't know how we'll manage it all.'

'I reckon I'm gonna eat the lot,' Fin mumbled over a mouthful while loading up his plate with more.

'Hey, go easy, kiddo.' Porsha rested a hand on his shoulder. 'We don't want a tummy ache before bed.'

'Why don't you and Lorenzo join us, Joyce? And Sofia?' Matteo suggested as inspiration struck. Helped along by Porsha's mention of "bed". 'In fact, why doesn't everyone come? Bring out the food in the staff kitchen, and we'll dine together tonight.'

'Oh, no, we wouldn't want to intrude on your— your time.' Strange that she stuttered over the 'your,' or was it the 'time'?

Had she been about to say something like special, private, *family* time?

He cleared his throat. 'I insist.'

The more chaperones, the better, especially those with eyes like Joyce.

'Yes, we'd love for you to join us,' Porsha said, taking his lead and showing no obvious surprise at the suggestion.

Joyce beamed. 'Well in that case...'

From there on, the dynamic changed as an impromptu party filled the terrace, all the staff appearing as another table was set. Enzo brought out his guitar and played, Sofia occasionally singing to an enraptured Fin, who, for a seven-year-old, was quite smitten. And *Dio*, Matteo could sympathise.

Because in spite of the noise, the companionship, the wise eyes and the distraction, the buzz remained.

The whole evening, as they ate, laughed, danced, chatted...

It built and built. And all because Matteo was happy. He realised that surrounded by his staff, with Porsha and Fin by his side, he *was* happy. He had all he needed. He hadn't thought of the game that had dominated most of his life. And thoughts of his father were muted by the love and warmth filling the terrace.

When Chef Paolo rolled out the dessert, his special tiramisu and an island favourite, everyone devoured it. Fin sneaking seconds when he thought they weren't looking. Everyone warned him that he wouldn't sleep a wink with all the caffeine and he was determined to prove them right.

It worked in Matteo's favour, too. After all, Fin being awake meant no more getting carried away that day…

But eventually, even Fin had to surrender. He fell asleep with his head in Porsha's lap, his body strewn across two chairs.

'I should carry him up,' Matteo said.

'It's okay, I can do it.'

'It's three flights.'

Her eyes sparked. 'Are you saying I'm weak, Matteo?'

Dio, he loved her fire. 'I wouldn't dare.'

Though they did concede it was easier for Matteo to lift him when she was still pinned by his head.

The boy roused as he scooped him up, snuggling into Matteo's neck with such trust his own throat closed over. 'Go back to sleep, kiddo.'

'Will you read me a story, Lucky?' he murmured.

Matteo met Porsha's gaze. 'Sure.'

He carried him to his room and helped him get ready for bed, settled him under the blanket with Ted and got in beside him.

'Ready?' Matteo said as Fin snuggled in close and the boy gave a sleepy nod.

Matteo started to read, barely aware of what he was saying as his heart continued with its chaotic beat. His head full of what-ifs and impossibilities.

Fin's snoring broke him out of it a few pages in and he closed the book. Looked down at the boy whose head rested on his chest. His peaceful breaths like a balm to Matteo's unsettled soul.

Only he didn't want to find peace in Fin's presence or Porsha's. Didn't want to depend on them. Because he'd never depended on anyone in that way. Not even his own mother.

And it wasn't fair. Not to Fin. Not to Porsha.

And there was something else at work…something so close to love that he shoved it aside. Dismissing it as nonsense. Something born of the lustful heat still pumping through his veins and messing with his head.

This was what happened when one forwent satisfaction at the precipice of such passion. It stuck around, building until one couldn't see past it…

Carefully he extracted himself from Fin's hold,

placed the book on the side and tucked the blanket to Fin's chin. Kissed his brow. *'Buona notte, tesorino.'*

'You've got that routine down pat.'

He startled at the whispered remark, saw Porsha in the shadow of the doorway to her room. How long had she been there?

Not long, or he would have sensed her presence, just like he always did. His body aware of hers long before his eyes caught sight.

He joined her on the threshold, realising when he spied the bed, *her* bed, that he should have encouraged her to the other exit into the outer hall. No extra temptation. No privacy too.

'He's wiped out.'

She nodded, her loving gaze on Fin. 'He's had an action-packed day, *another* great day thanks to you…' She lifted that same gaze to him, all the emotion remaining and stealing his breath. 'What does it mean? I got the goodnight bit, but *tesorino*?'

A smile touched his lips at the happier memories of old. 'It's what my mother used to call me— little treasure.'

Her lashes flickered, her lips curved. 'That's sweet.'

It was sweet. It was deep. It was meaningful. Everything he swore he would never be with another, yet here he was.

'What are we doing, Porsha?'

Her eyes narrowed to slits. 'We're doing what you said we should do, we're having fun.'

He closed the door with an imperceptible click.

'I don't mean us as a…group.' He'd almost said 'family,' the word cropping up too often. 'I mean you and me. Because you *know* me, you know me better than anyone.'

'I'd like to think I do.'

'Then you know what this is and what it can never be.'

'Yes, Matteo. I know you. I know what this is. And I want you. Right here in my present.'

'But then what?'

'Then nothing. This is a holiday fling, for the duration of this break, then we go back home and revert to how things were.'

'You think it's that simple?'

Because nothing about sex with Porsha was simple. And it terrified him that he could get this wrong.

'Why wouldn't it be?'

'What about Fin?'

'We just need to be careful.'

Careful. He could do that. Couldn't he?

'And in a few weeks,' she continued, 'he'll be back in school, I'll be back at work, and you can go back to your life. Everything will be as it was.'

'Not everything though, Porsha.' He stroked her hair from her face, cupped her cheek. Unable to stomach the idea that she would go back to being the same overworked, overstretched parent, with no time for her and Fin. 'Please, don't let it be *just* the same. Carve out time for you both. Live a little. Keep the balance.'

She gave a small smile. 'I will. And maybe when you're around, you could sometimes join us? For dinner, a trip to the park…a game of chess?'

He traced her lower lip with his thumb, so many other ideas burning through him that couldn't happen. 'I'd like that.'

'And then you have Canada…'

He stilled. He hadn't thought that far ahead. He loved it out there. Loved the snow. The exhilarating slopes. The climate. But right now, it had nothing on this.

And that was telling enough.

'I don't know, Porsha.'

'You don't know?' She surprised him with a soft laugh. 'I don't believe this.'

'What?'

'Is it possible we've had a personality swap while here?'

He frowned. 'A personality swap…?'

'You're still fretting, worrying over the future?'

'I'm sorry, it's just…' He broke away from her, thrust both hands through his hair as he strode to the window. Looked out over the island and the sea. All at peace. A peace he wanted for himself too, but not when it was so dependent on others.

'I care, Porsha. I care about you and Fin, and I don't want to hurt either of you.'

She came up behind him, her hand on his shoulder forcing him to turn.

'You'd never intentionally hurt us, Matteo. I know that.'

'And what about unintentionally?'

'This need I have for you, just here—' she touched a hand to her abdomen, fisted the black silk of her dress '—*it* hurts and I want you to take it away.'

He couldn't respond. His head, heart, body… they were all at war.

She released the fabric only to lower her hands to the hem, drying up his mouth, silencing his mind.

'You can tell me to stop and I will…'

She eased it up and his betraying gaze dipped. His need soaring with every inch she exposed. Her svelte thighs that had been locked around him hours ago. The gentle swell of her hips that now bore a revealing strip of pink lace. Her taut stomach that spoke of the pulsating need she had trapped beneath…

Dio mio.

'But you did promise me.' She lifted the dress over her head. 'And I do owe you.'

She let it fall from her fingers and he drank her in. Top to toe and back again, his journey cut short by her bra. *That* bra.

A tight chuckle erupted. 'It survived Fin's antics then?'

'Yes.' She trailed a hand over one curve, fingertips teasing at the bra's lace edge. 'And since it brought us together, I figured I owed it a special outing.'

'Minus the garden fence?'

She nodded. 'No more dividing line, Matteo. It's time to call in the debt—'

With a curse, he tugged her to him, kissing her until there was only one thing on his mind—to make good on his promise.

Over and over and over again.

CHAPTER FOURTEEN

PORSHA GAVE A heartfelt sigh and threw herself back on the bed, starfish style—Fin would be proud.

Almost three weeks on the island, and two weeks since she'd made the decision to live each day to the full. Days packed with thrilling new experiences. On and off the water. In and out of the bedroom.

She never saw the Jet Skis again. Matteo hadn't made a show of it. They'd simply disappeared overnight, and for that she was grateful. Because no amount of growing as a person and healing from her past could see her going anywhere near one of those.

She owed him so much, her heart an ever-expanding balloon of gratitude. Not just for her own happiness and that of Fin's, but for the peace he had brought them too. A way of living in harmony together. Less dishing out of the discipline and more of the loving gestures and permissive fun.

True quality time.

So much so that the idea of moving forward as

a family of two back in England no longer felt so daunting.

Granted, a family of three would be perfect. But she dismissed the picture as soon as it presented itself because though she was done obsessing over the risks, she wasn't so far done with it that she didn't know a bridge too far to cross. Matteo had made his views on love clear, and those views hadn't changed. No matter how much he cared for her and Fin, it could never evolve into the kind of love she wanted.

She pressed her lips together, the ache in her heart too deep to ignore.

How could a man so caring, so thoughtful, so kind, close himself off from love and be happy?

Leave it alone. Take what he's willing to give and make that enough.

And she knew her head was right. Because he wanted her, and that in itself had her flying high.

He was Matteo De Luca. 'Lucky Luca', a football superstar. He dated super models and actresses and the world's most beautiful women, yet here he was with her.

But you're beautiful too.

Sassy was in her head again. Her sister's frustration that Porsha was too pessimistic in every walk of life, her looks included, a constant bugbear. But Porsha had always preferred the term *realistic*. Though she was starting to see that Sassy had a point. Sassy and her parents and her colleagues who saw her working too much, playing too little.

But it had taken Matteo to open her eyes to it.

'Aunt Porsha, breakfast is ready!' Fin swung his head round the door and then skipped off.

Porsha followed, leaving the remnants of worry behind as she lost herself in the beauty of the fort. Its charm increasing with each passing day.

'Signor De Luca is on a call, he'll join you shortly,' Joyce said as Porsha stepped out onto the terrace. The table she was fussing over beautifully arranged. A continental spread fit for a king and a floral vase overflowing with colour from the island. She'd miss this when they returned to England later in the week. Miss this and so much more.

'Amazing as always, Joyce, thank you.'

'It's my pleasure.'

Porsha plucked a grape and popped it in her mouth, her eyes drifting to the sea, but her thoughts were all on Matteo and what excitement today would bring.

'You look super happy, Aunt Porsha!' Fin announced, surprising her out of her thoughts. He sat at the table beside her, legs swinging, plate full, head upturned as he scrutinised her face. As though he really meant it and really wanted her to know it.

'The boy's right,' Joyce said, clutching an empty tray to her chest. 'You're glowing.'

And she knew why she was glowing. Her feelings for Matteo were swelling out of her control, blooming from the inside out. And there was nothing she could do about it.

'As is Matteo…'

She almost choked on her grape. Joyce's words causing her pulse to spike and her throat to close over.

'It's nice,' the woman assured her with a smile, her blue eyes soft and…and loving. For her, for Matteo, for whatever she thought existed between Porsha *and* Matteo. Oh no, she couldn't think… she couldn't know…

'*Really* nice,' she added, turning to walk back inside, seemingly oblivious to what she had stirred up.

Porsha hurried after her. 'Joyce?'

She paused on the threshold. 'Yes, dear.'

Porsha swallowed. What should she say? What did she want to say?

'Is it *that* obvious?' That for all they'd tried to keep their stolen kisses by day and rendezvous by night a secret, the entire household was aware. And if they were aware, did that mean…?

'I don't want…' Porsha's eyes drifted to Fin outside, now tucking in with glee.

'It's obvious for us who are older and wiser… and we couldn't be happier. But the boy isn't naive, he knows enough. And he's happy too. Just look at him.'

Porsha *was* looking. And she was seeing. And she was praying it wasn't because Fin believed his aunt and Matteo were getting it on!

Joyce headed into the kitchen and Porsha followed on her heels. 'Why did you say, "it's nice" like that?'

Because when Joyce said it, Porsha got the distinct impression that the older women thought there was more than just sex between them. More than sex on *both* sides.

'Because it's nice to know that he isn't as closed off to love as we always feared.' She slipped the tray away and started moving the dirty pans from the hob to the sink, not once breaking step as Porsha's heart pricked up. 'He had a tough beginning, what with his father and mother being forced to part ways, and all that resentment within the family. It couldn't have been healthy growing up in a home riddled with all that hate.'

'You know about his past?'

'We all do, dear. Lorenzo is his mother's cousin.'

'Lorenzo! *Your* Lorenzo?'

'Oh yes. You didn't know? Well, why would you when the man doesn't like to talk about his family or his past.' She set the taps going and added soap to the sink. 'But he did right by my Lorenzo, gave him a job when he needed one.'

'I thought Matteo didn't speak to any of his family.'

'There aren't many left to speak to, save for Lorenzo and his father.'

'Matteo's father—you know who he is?'

Now Joyce looked uncomfortable, biting the inside of her lips as she pointedly ignored Porsha.

'Joyce?'

'Leave it, love.' She turned off the taps and started to wash up. 'I think I've said enough already.'

'Then tell me, how did Matteo and Lorenzo come together? I thought he'd cut all ties with his family in Italy.'

Joyce paused, flicked her a look. 'He told you that much?'

Porsha nodded and Joyce gave a wistful smile. 'It's good that he has told you some of it. A good sign that he hasn't dismissed his past altogether.'

'And Lorenzo?'

'It was a long time ago…' Joyce returned to her washing up but this time, she carried on talking. 'Matteo was in Italy with his team and he took a detour. He came looking for answers, wanting to understand what had happened. He only had his mother's version and the bitter view of his grandparents. I think he wanted someone else to affirm it all. Lorenzo was the man he came to, and my Lorenzo confirmed it.

'But when Matteo asked him of his father, Lorenzo tried to tell him differently. Tried to convince him that his father was a good man, innocent and as broken by it all as his mother had been. But Matteo wouldn't hear it. He saw his father's new family as reason enough to believe it hadn't been the same for him. That his father must have been relieved to have been saved the shame and difficulty of being young parents in a community that would have openly shunned them.'

Joyce shook her head, her shoulders slumping with the weight of her tale. 'Anyway, they stayed in contact, and a couple of years later, when I was pregnant with Sofia and the hotel Lorenzo worked for went bust, Matteo offered him a job in one of his establishments. Then when he bought the island, he offered us a job and a home for life here.'

That was so Matteo. Thoughtful and caring, even as he refused to give his own father the benefit of the doubt.

'So Lorenzo knows where his father is now?'

Joyce coloured, busying herself with the dishes, and Porsha reached out to touch her arm. 'Joyce?'

She stopped, her head lifting to meet Porsha's gaze as she admitted, 'Lorenzo sends updates to his father—personal updates. Not the kind of fabricated nonsense the press likes to put out there. And nothing too private. Just enough to reassure him of how he's doing. He's always cared, love. When Matteo bought the island, his father sold everything on the mainland and sank it all into a tiny restaurant on the coast of Capri. He moved his family there so that he could look out over his other, hoping that one day...well, you know...'

'Then why didn't he reach out himself? He's had years to get to know his son, to show him that he cares.'

'Those are questions only he can answer. But Lorenzo trusts him, and if Lorenzo trusts him, I do too. But please, don't tell Matteo of this. He's found his peace with Lorenzo, and I fear this could come between them.'

'I won't, of course I won't.'

'I haven't given up hope that someday, something will happen to change things. And maybe that something is you.'

'Me?'

Joyce nodded. 'Don't underestimate the power of love, dear...'

'Love?' Porsha's cheeks coloured and she shook her head. 'I'm sorry, Joyce, I think you put too much stock into what this is between us.'

'And perhaps, you put in too little...' Her eyes sparkled. 'Now, *go eat* before Fin devours the lot!'

Porsha returned to the table in a daze. Was Joyce right? Was there more going on between them? Enough for her to try and fix Matteo just a little? Not change him too much, because to her mind, though his spontaneity, adrenaline-seeking, risk-taking ways made him too much like her family, they were also a part of him. Part of what made him joyous and fun and wonderful beyond measure. Just like her family she was starting to realise. Thanks to him.

But to change his relationship with love…to build upon the qualities he already possessed?

As for how she felt towards him, she wasn't travelling down that road. Not just yet, not when the future was so uncertain and she'd promised not to dwell on it too.

'Ah, there you are!' Matteo's face lit up as he rose from the table. He must have returned while she was talking to Joyce. 'I was worried I'd tired you out with all the activities and you'd gone back to bed.'

The way his eyes danced—activities definitely being code for bedroom antics—had her grinning in spite of all that Joyce had stirred up.

'Not a chance.'

'Glad to hear it because I have a plan for today.'

Fin's ears pricked up. 'Are we going to try out water-skiing?'

Porsha's heart leapt, she wasn't ready for any kind of skiing.

'Let's just stick to the SUP boarding for now, kid. We've only just got your aunt on one board. Two skinny ones…' He shook his head, adding at Fin's overly dramatic pout, 'Let's save it for next time you're out here.'

'There's gonna be a next time?' Fin exclaimed, wide-eyed. Porsha's sentiments exactly!

'I'd like to think so, if your aunt is up for it.'

She gave a weak smile. 'Sure. Of course.'

His eyes narrowed. 'Everything okay?'

'Never better. What was it you had planned?' she asked, quick to change the subject.

He scanned her face, wanting to be sure she was okay, and her heart warmed with her smile. A smile he then returned.

'How do you both feel about a trip to Capri today? A friend of mine called this morning, Rodrigo. He's visiting with his son, Danny, a year older than you, Fin. We thought we could do the local stadium, have a kickabout, grab something to eat…?'

Fin whooped his approval, but Porsha was too busy with her thoughts. A visit to Capri? The island where his father was…

Could Porsha see for herself what kind of a man he was, get a feel for the truth and do something to help Matteo heal as he had helped her? Was this how she could repay him? Do as Joyce thought possible and bring father and son back together again?

'Porsha?'

'Hmm?'

He gave a bemused frown. 'You were away with the fairies…'

'What did I miss?'

'A trip to Capri. The idea has Fin's vote, what about you?'

She wrinkled her nose. 'I can't say a kickabout

in a stadium with all that testosterone flying about is my idea of fun. Taking a stroll along its historic streets and indulging in a bit of shopping, on the other hand… I could do with a few colourful pieces to add to my wardrobe.'

He grinned his approval. 'That's settled then. I'll get Enzo to ready the yacht.'

And she'd get Joyce to give her the details she needed…

Her belly gave a nervous flutter and she plonked herself down at the table. Filled her plate. Not that she had much appetite now. She was too preoccupied with the day ahead.

It may not go to plan, but true to her new self, she wasn't going to sit here and debate every eventuality until the nerves won out.

Above all, she owed it to Matteo to at least try… *and* buy an outfit to blow his mind.

CHAPTER FIFTEEN

'I THINK IT'S a great idea, Lucky. Inspired, even.'

'That's Porsha for you...' Matteo said, his gaze on Fin and Danny out on the pitch.

They had an audience of three. Matteo and Rodrigo, up in the stadium seats, and the groundskeeper who had granted them access, supervising from the sidelines below.

Being rich and famous occasionally had its perks.

'A footie centre for troubled kids run by former players... Why didn't we come up with it?'

'Damned if I know...too busy sticking our heads in the sand I guess.'

Rodrigo gave a low chuckle, leaned back. 'Women do that.'

'Do what?'

'Force us to look up every now and then.'

Matteo gave a non-committal grunt that had his friend chuckling again.

'So...now that the lads are out there, you going to tell me what's really going on?'

Matteo pulled a packet of nuts out of his pocket and ripped them open.

'I don't know what you're talking about.'

He offered the packet to Rodrigo who waved it away.

'Pull the other one, mate. Leo's been on the blower telling all who will listen that they're living with you now.'

Matteo threw some nuts in his mouth, chewed them over as he refused to rise to his friend's words.

'They're not living with me. They're my neighbours.'

'Not here, they ain't.'

'No, here they're my guests.'

'Guests, right. So you're not sleeping with her?'

Matteo choked on a stray nut.

He's got you there.

Rodrigo grinned. 'Your silence says it all.'

'No, it doesn't!'

'Hey, since when have you gotten all uppity and defensive about who you're sleeping with?'

'Porsha's different.'

'In what way?'

Yes, in what way, Matteo?

Hell, he didn't know. He just knew she was different.

'She has a child, for a start.'

Yes, blame your messed up feelings on Fin... and not on the fact that you're struggling to see a future without her.

'And he's a great kid, he could do a lot worse than you for a father figure...'

'I'm not his father.'

'I didn't say you were. I'm just saying—'

'I know what you were saying, but leave it, Rodrigo.'

'I fail to see what your problem is. From where I'm sitting, you have it all. A woman you can live with and still smile, and a boy who adores the ground you walk on.'

'She's not my woman.'

'The ex still around?'

'What? No. Fin's her nephew, her sister's child. His mother died a couple of years ago in a nasty accident, and he was put in the care of his aunt. No one knows who his father is.'

'Wow, poor kid. Poor Porsha. That's a hell of a lot to go through.'

'And I'm trying to help them through it.'

'Which is real decent of you. But while you're helping them through it, maybe you ought to take a time out and consider where you sit in all of this. Because soon enough, this will be public knowledge, and you're going to need to have an answer at the ready for the press. And "she's my neighbor" ain't going to cut it.'

Matteo swallowed a curse. He knew Rodrigo was right.

But he couldn't put a label on what he and Porsha were, because every label he was willing to give just felt wrong.

'I don't mean to pry, you know that, right? You're

my best mate. All I'm saying is that regardless of what Leo is banding about, you're different. You've changed. You've texted her—what?—twenty times since you've been out with me. Checked your phone a whole lot more. And you're never this pensive about anything, unless we were talking strategy and football, and let's face it, those days are over.'

'Cheers for the reminder.'

He waited for the usual ache, the hollow pang, but…nothing.

'I'm serious, mate, there's something about you, and it reminds me of when I met Janey. And I'm only saying this because I'm scared you'll run from it. You want my advice?'

Matteo choked out a laugh. 'Hell no.'

'Tough. Don't waste your time running, because it'll catch up with you eventually. And the sooner you accept it and move forward, the better.'

'And I say again, you don't know what you're talking about.'

But even to his own ears, Matteo's words lacked any real conviction. His gut taking a roll that had him resealing the nuts and stowing them away.

''Course I don't. Only been married ten years and counting.'

'Ten years? Has it *really* been that long?' He'd given it a year. Two tops. Then Danny had come along, followed by his little sister, Flo, and still

Matteo had thought the end would come. How wrong could he have been?

'Time flies when you're having fun, right?'

'Yeah…' But then Rodrigo came from a loving home with a large family, it stood to reason he would make it work. He knew what it was to love, how to love. What did Matteo know?

He'd had grandparents who resented him, a father willing to disown him and a mother unwilling to let such a man go.

He would never be as cold as the former two or as blind as the latter.

And so, he would go it alone…just as soon as they were back on British soil and not a second before. Because for all he may fear such a heartfelt connection, he couldn't deny the happiness it had brought him thus far.

Fin's goal-fuelled cheer echoed through the stadium and Matteo smiled—because it wasn't just about himself. In fact, he was way down on his own priority list.

It was for the happiness he had brought them too—Fin and Porsha.

A happiness they were long overdue and thriving on now.

But for how long?

Porsha didn't like lying to Matteo. So the second he and Fin left her at Capri's Marina Grande, she headed for its infamous shopping triangle—another detail Joyce had given her—eagerly taking in her fresh surroundings.

From the yachts and multi-coloured fishermen homes to the ancient bougainvillea-covered buildings and the cinematic car-free streets, Capri oozed beauty, wealth and charm. It was easy to see why the rich and famous flocked here. And why closet historians like herself would love to stick around and discover more, but she told herself next time.

Just as Matteo had promised Fin, there would be a next time to do more.

As for the shopping, it bedazzled!

She hadn't been clothes shopping in forever and this was hardly the place for the unacquainted. An abundance of styles, colours, brands, luxury boutique items, high-end designers, bespoke one-offs…all at an eye-watering cost. She was starting to wonder how she'd choose something when a dress in a window caught her eye.

Red, daring and bold—right up Matteo's street! Hers too, now that she was being honest with herself.

The style, according to the shop assistant who'd hurried out to greet her, was *made* for her. The halter neck and short cut leaving enough of her petite frame on show. The delicate fabric clinging to her curves in all the right places. Striking enough to be considered sexy but also classy.

Especially when paired with the diamanté

heeled sandals the shop assistant delighted in up-selling her.

Porsha smothered a wince as she handed over her credit card, reminding herself this was a one-off and the reward when Matteo saw her in it… *oh, yes,* definitely worth it.

Purchases wrapped and bagged, she headed back outside and straight into a souvenir shop. If she was treating herself, she was treating Matteo and Fin too. She snapped up two matching leather bracelets. Simple but, oh, so sweet, and she knew the men in her life would appreciate them.

Happy she'd done the shopping she'd promised, she pulled out her phone, double-checked her direction and hurried off. It was getting late, and she didn't want to rush this meeting. If her plan went how she wanted, today could give Matteo and his father a fresh start…

She had Lorenzo and Joyce's blessing, and the two were primed to come to her aid that evening. Now she just needed the people at the heart of her plan to come together.

In the hustle and bustle, she almost missed the quiet little side street she needed. Taking a turn at the last minute, she came to a halt before a restaurant.

Flowers trailed out of baskets overhead and flourished in pots either side of the entrance. It was homely and quaint, the sign above giving the impression that it had been there for as long as the street itself and lovingly maintained...

Trattoria la Familiare.

Porsha didn't speak much Italian, but she recognised 'family' when she saw it. Her heart swooned, and she rechecked the map on her phone. This was it. This was his father's place.

'Can I help you?'

Porsha looked up to see a tall young woman in the doorway, probably a year or two younger than Porsha herself. Dark hair tied back at the nape, kind brown eyes...

'Erm, yes, I'm looking for Roberto Canali?'

The other woman smiled. 'You'll be looking for my father, then. Come this way.'

Her father. This was Matteo's *half-sister.* Porsha swallowed. Now she felt like she was overstepping, meeting his sister before he had, meeting his family, but what choice was there when he refused to cross the divide?

'Signorina?'

Porsha shook herself out of her stupor and followed her inside.

You owe it to him, remember?

And knowing that he had a half-sister he'd never met... Porsha would do anything to have her sister back, to have another sibling to walk through life with. Matteo didn't need to be alone. Not any more.

Even if he didn't want her in his future, he should at least have this.

His family.

Matteo was surprised to see Lorenzo and Joyce on board the yacht when he returned with Fin in the late afternoon. 'What are you two doing here?'

'Enzo brought us over on the speedboat. We fancied some sunset fishing and thought we'd see if Fin wanted to join us.'

'I'm not sure, I thought maybe Porsha and I would take him to dinner.'

'I thought we could do dinner, just the two of us.'

The woman herself appeared and Matteo had to grip the deck's handrail to stop from staggering back.

'*Porsha*?'

Only it didn't look like Porsha. Not the Porsha he was used to.

This Porsha looked like a siren. The kind of siren who according to legend had once lured Ulysses into the Faraglioni across the way.

'You might want to close your mouth, dear,' Joyce murmured under her breath. 'Else you'll catch a fly.'

He snapped his jaw shut, and Fin dashed forward, coming to a stop a stride away from his aunt. 'You look a million bucks!'

Porsha smiled, the most dazzling, eye-twinkling smile. 'I'll do then?'

Matteo came up behind Fin. 'You'll more than do, *sei stupenda.*' And unthinking he reached out, one hand on her hip as he leaned in and kissed her cheek, whispering against her ear, *'Sei bellissima. Non vedo l'ora di divorarti.'*

Her cheeks warmed, her eyes questioning his meaning, but it was written in his face. *I can't wait to devour you.* And he couldn't.

'Are you ready for dinner?' she murmured. 'I've booked somewhere…'

'Give me ten minutes to freshen up and I'll be right with you.'

She gave a tremulous smile, which he put down to being uncertain in red. 'This dress is perfect for you. *You* are perfect.'

And just like that, her smile solidified. 'Before you go, I have something for you.'

She reached inside her purse and took out two leather bracelets, identical save for the size.

'Wow, is one for me?' Fin blurted.

'I thought you'd like a piece of Capri to take home with you.' She smiled as she handed one to Matteo and slid the other over Fin's outstretched wrist. 'Do you like it?'

'It's so cool! We're twinning, Lucky!'

'So we are.' His smile was oddly choked, his chest both warm and tight as he fastened the leather around his wrist and angled it for a better look.

'Enzo will run us back to the island after and we can take Fin with us,' Joyce said, reminding him that they were still there witnessing it all. 'Leave you with the yacht for the night…?'

'That would be great,' Porsha surprised him by answering first, the look she exchanged with Joyce speaking volumes. Volumes of what, though, he wasn't sure. It was like the two had hatched a plan only they were privy to.

But if that plan was to permit Porsha the perfect evening of seduction, he was all for it. He could worry about the bracelet and the bond and the ever-swelling boulder in his chest later.

CHAPTER SIXTEEN

'WHERE ARE WE HEADING?'

She smiled up at him as they climbed the winding streets of Capri, the odd look from passers-by reminding her of who he was and why she likely shouldn't have her arm hooked in his. But if it didn't bother him…

'I thought we could take a stroll before dinner.'

He chuckled. 'Like you haven't walked enough today?'

'When you're in a place like this, you can never walk enough…'

In a place like this, with a man like him…

Especially when he was like he was—an extra spring in his step, an extra spark in his gaze.

'You seem more excitable than usual. Did you have a good time with Rodrigo?'

'Yeah, it's been a while. He's been busy helping with the family firm, finding his own feet after football. I told him your idea for a youth centre…'

Her heart gave a jolt. 'You did?'

Did that mean he was seriously considering

it? He hadn't mentioned it since, and she hadn't pressed because...well, she'd been too busy losing herself in everything else between them.

'He loved it. Said he'd be up for investing and chipping in with the sessions too. It really was a great idea, Porsha. Once I find a venue, we can take it from there, start with one, get it right and branch out. The more locations, the more kids we can help.'

Tears filled her eyes. 'I don't know what to say.'

'Well, don't cry!' He reached an arm around her, squeezed her to him. 'Be proud that I've seen the light.'

She gave a choked laugh. If only he could see the light with his father so easily.

She fell quiet, nerves a rampant wriggle in her gut, making it hard to concentrate. He was so happy, riding high on the changes he was already making, and here she was, unbeknownst to him, pressing for more. Was it too much all at once?

'Are you happy, Matteo?' she asked, hesitating. Because the youth centre would give him a new purpose, something to plough his energy into, but it wouldn't give him a home, a family to call his own. And without that, could he *be* happy? Truly content?

She thought of his therapy, the addiction he was working through. Would he always be working through it? Wasn't that the way with addicts?

He gave her an odd look. 'Is it not obvious?'

'I'd like to think you are.' She smiled softly. 'I'd like to think this holiday has meant as much to you as it has to me and Fin.'

'It's been one of my most memorable stays on the island,' he said carefully.

'Would you change anything?'

He stopped walking and pulled her round to face him. To their left, the sun dipped behind the ocean, its soft glow enhancing everything it touched—the boats in the marina, the bougainvillea-covered buildings and the ancient path—but it had nothing on him. His dark shirt open at the collar, his equally dark hair carefully groomed and swept back off his face and his eyes, darker than the shirt he wore and full of desire. For her.

'Not for a moment.'

Her mouth parted, but she couldn't find the words. Nothing felt good enough, strong enough, and then he took away the need with his mouth. Brushing a kiss over her lips as he cupped her face and held her there.

'If I wasn't convinced that you were heading for the hangry stage, I'd take you back to the yacht and make this stay all the more amazing.'

She gave him a weak smile. Weak with want and weak with what was to come. Maybe she'd called this wrong, maybe she should have taken them for food somewhere first, but the idea of eating anything when she was so nervous, so uncertain...

She took his hand from her cheek, held it as she led him onwards. They were close. So very close. It was true what Joyce had said, that all his father had to do was step out of his home and he could see Matteo's island.

'Shall we head into the town?' He started to tug her in the other direction, and she shook her head.

'I've seen the town, I want to go this way…' She pressed on, but Matteo wasn't so keen to move with her any more, and after a few more steps, he forced them to a standstill. 'What's wrong?'

He pocketed his hands, looked back the other way. To where the town was still bustling and the restaurant tables spilled out onto the streets. 'There's nothing to see up here.'

He was right, it was quieter. Homes were interspersed with the odd eatery and shopfront. Fewer pedestrians, less noise. But that wasn't what he was afraid of, and she stepped forward, touched her palm to his arm. 'Matteo?'

He didn't look at her. *'Si?'*

'Why don't you want to go up there?'

His brow furrowed, his eyes now dark with the storm brewing.

'Matt—'

'Why are you so keen *I* do?'

The *I* was telling enough.

'I thought—I wanted—'

'You know, don't you?' His head snapped around, his eyes spearing her. 'You *know* who lives up there.'

Her throat clammed up and she nodded, wet her lips. 'I do. I—Joyce told me.'

'Joyce? How could she…? Lorenzo!'

'But please don't be mad at them, they only want what's best for you and—'

'What's best for *me* is to get as far away from that man as possible.'

He took a step in the opposite direction.

'I met him today,' Porsha blurted, desperate to make him stop. Desperate to make him see. 'Him and his—your family.'

He stilled, his shoulders hunching around his ears.

'They were—'

'That man is no family of mine!' he ground out, spinning back to face her. 'Not him and not anyone else foolish enough to make him such.'

He strode back up to her with eyes that burned her very soul.

'What gave you the right?!'

She opened her mouth, but nothing would come. Not in the face of the words she had feared the most. The words she had thrown at herself on the threshold of his father's restaurant…

But just as she had then, she looked to her heart, the reason that it gave and took strength from it.

'Because you deserve to have a family, Matteo. A family that loves you and you can love in return.'

He shook his head, his body vibrating with the anger still rolling.

'You had *no* right to see him. No right at all.'

'Maybe that's true. But you've done so much to change me for the better, I hoped to—'

He laughed, the sound mocking and cold and unrecognisable. 'Oh, don't tell me, you hoped to change me in return?'

'I hoped I could help you heal,' she whispered, heartbroken to see the man she had come to care for so deeply in such pain. To be the trigger and now the object of it, too. 'I wanted to meet the man you claimed abandoned you. I wanted to know whether he was a good man worthy of knowing you. Worthy of being given a chance at a relationship that was taken away from the two of you all those years ago.'

'You are delusional, Porsha. When have I *ever* given you a hint that I want this?'

'It's not always about what you want, but what you need.'

'And you think I *need* to come face to face with the man who ruined my life, ruined my *mother's* life?'

'I think you need to hear his side of it, yes.'

'Matteo?'

The male voice, thick and gruff, came from behind them. Wide-eyed and ashen-faced, Matteo spun towards it as his father came out of the shadows.

'Get the hell away from me!'

The older man flinched. 'Please, son, just give me…'

'Don't you "son" me.' Matteo backed up, head shaking.

'Please…' Porsha stepped forward, one hand reaching out. 'Speak to—'

He spun into her. 'And you can get the hell away from me too.'

'You don't mean—'

'How *dare* you tell me what I need, what I mean,' he spat out as she stumbled back. 'I was wrong, Porsha! You *should* think before you act, because then you wouldn't have played such a foolish and devious move as this.'

Tears spiked, her heart breaking in two. 'Please, I just wanted to—'

'Since you are such good friends with Lorenzo, he can see to it that you get back to London safely.'

'But Fin and—'

'Tell him I had to leave with Rodrigo.'

'Please don't take it out on her.' His father stepped forward, his Italian accent heavy, dark eyes so like his son's, pleading with him to listen.

'And you—' Matteo thrust a finger out, backing up at the same time '—come anywhere near me again, and I'll see to it that you regret it!'

And then he was gone, running through the streets and the people, and she could do nothing but watch as her heart left with him. Because in that moment, Porsha realised with absolute certainty that she was in love with him.

Irrevocably and undeniably.

And whatever they had shared, it was over. All because she couldn't leave well enough alone.

Matteo hadn't asked for any of this. He hadn't asked to meet his father. He hadn't asked for her to fall in love with him. His heart wasn't open to love and maybe it never would be.

By his own admission, Matteo was a man you had fun with. He wasn't the man you brought home to your parents as future husband material.

Though hers would've adored him. Adored him because he'd brought her life balance, brought her wild side to the surface, no matter how small, and given her the fun she'd lacked.

Sassy would have adored him too. Just as Porsha utterly adored him.

Well, not quite. Because she was head over heels in love with him.

And now she'd lost him.

CHAPTER SEVENTEEN

One week later

'WHY ARE YOU ANGRY?'

'Because she *betrayed* me,' he blurted into the phone, Isabella's measured question pushing him over the edge. They'd been over it enough times already. Surely it had to be obvious by now.

'How did she betray you?'

Was his therapist for *real*?

'Because she took my greatest fear and exploited it.'

'How?'

'She took me to see my father!' He strode up to his bedroom window and glared out at the Tyrrhenian Sea and the island of Capri. 'Of all the men in all the world...'

'She took you to see the one who has hurt you the most.'

'Certamente!'

'And she told you that she did it because she wanted him to have the opportunity to explain and—'

'We've been through all this a thousand times, Isabella.'

She blew out a breath, loud enough to reach him down the line. Did his therapist just *sigh* at him?

'What is your greatest fear, Matteo?'

'You know what my fear is. Hell, you were the one who helped me uncover it.'

'You fear being abandoned, but your father wasn't walking away from you in Capri, was he? According to Porsha, he was there to speak to you and explain. Because she believes he cares, and she believes it would help you to hear him out.'

'*Si.*'

'So, in what way could she have taken your greatest fear, your fear of being abandoned, and exploited it?'

Matteo fell silent, the answer flickering to life in his gut and spreading as quick as wildfire.

'Who were you afraid of losing in that moment, Matteo?'

He shook his head. Not wanting to accept it and accepting it all the same.

'It doesn't matter, because she's gone anyway, and you as my therapist should be glad of it.'

'Why would I be glad?'

'Because she was just another addiction, something to crave and need and want to the extent that the past week has been a living hell without her. I can't sleep. I can't eat. I can't think!'

'And why do you think that is, Matteo?'

'I just told you, I'm an addict.'

'No. You told me what you want me to hear, what you want yourself to hear. Go deeper, Matteo.'

'No.' He sounded like a sullen child being told to do something he didn't want to do.

'Why?'

He didn't answer.

'You know...' she began softly '...some of the greatest ballads of our time talk of love and addiction in the same breath. Why do you think that is?'

Matteo squeezed his eyes shut and forked his fingers through his hair, gripped his head. Was it possible that for all his claims that he would never fall for someone, never risk the fear of losing another, or give another such power over him...that...

'I have to go.'

'We have another ten minutes and I—'

'I know what I have to do.'

He hung up the phone and lifted his head, taking in the island once more and the man he needed to confront. Because if he wanted to look to the future and what he wanted for it, he needed to put his past to bed...for good.

'Porsha, can you comment on your relationship with Lucky Luca?'

'Ms Lang, is it true you're dating your neighbour?'

'Is Matteo De Luca the boy's true father?'

That last one had Porsha almost swing for the reporter, but Fin was tucked under her coat, and it was taking all she had to keep him covered up with one arm while the other shoved them out of the way. All so she could get to her front door.

She'd hoped some other story would have caught their attention by now, but it seemed when the gossip was about someone as notorious as Matteo dating someone as everyday as Porsha, it bore no expiry date.

Though it had only been a few days since the news had broken, it was more that it *felt* like so much longer.

She slammed the door closed on the verbal assault and cameras, engaged all the locks as Fin loped off to the family room, taking it in stride.

Not that he should have to. She took a breath, calming her pulse and her temper, and followed him in.

'I'm sorry about all this, kiddo.'

He shrugged. 'It doesn't bother me. Everyone at school thinks I'm famous now.'

He gave her a brave smile, but she knew he was putting on a front. Trying to be okay for her. Something he should never have to do. She was the responsible adult, she was the one who was supposed to be protecting him. Instead she'd brought all this chaos to his door. Literally. And all because she'd been so selfish, so foolish and thoughtless.

'You know they all think you're his girlfriend...'

He was looking at his phone now, scrolling down the screen.

'You shouldn't listen to them,' she said, shrugging out of her coat and hanging it in the hallway. 'They talk a load of nonsense.'

'Sometimes, but not always.'

'What do you mean "not always"?'

She re-entered the room and he lifted his phone to her. Filling the screen was a photo she'd stared at far too much for her own sanity. The one that had triggered all the reports. Snapped in Capri, it showed her and Matteo at sunset, her hair and red dress shifting on the breeze as he cupped her face and kissed her. The loving moment captured so perfectly, anyone would think they'd staged it.

She tried to smile over the heartache, but it felt as false as Fin's had been.

'The headlines suck though,' he blurted, bringing the phone back to him. 'Has Lucky Luca Finally Hit the "Lurve" Jackpot? Matteo De Luca, Lucky in Love! Who's the Woman Lucky Enough to Steal Lucky Luca's Heart? Has Lucky Luca Been Hiding a Family All This Time? Any reporter good at their job would know you're not my mum and he isn't my father.'

The sadness in that one statement, the grief it barely concealed, had Porsha rushing to the sofa and pulling him into her side. He'd lost his mum and now he'd lost Matteo too. She couldn't hate herself more.

'I'm sorry, darling. So sorry.'

'I'm only sorry that you're sad and that Matteo and you aren't friends any more. I thought he was nice and that he liked us.'

'He did like us. He does like you.'

'But not you?'

She nipped her lip, chose her words carefully. 'I upset him. I did something I shouldn't have.'

'Did you say you were sorry?'

Had she? She couldn't remember, for as much as she played that conversation over and over in her head, the finer details blurred with the anguish of losing him and her guilt.

'I'm not sure.'

He pressed her away, looked up, eyes bright with hope. 'Then that's what you need to do. Like you tell me all the time, when you hurt someone, even if it's by accident, you say you're sorry.'

'You're right, honey. I know you're right. And I will, just as soon as he gets home.'

Because she had to try. She couldn't leave things like this.

'When will that be?'

She pulled him back in, kissed his head and tried to ignore the ache within. 'I don't know.'

And who was to say he would come back? He had the money to live anywhere he wanted, so why would he choose to come back and live next door to her? The one woman who had hurt him so deeply?

The doorbell rang and she smothered a curse. Why couldn't they just bugger off and leave them in peace? Leave her heart in peace? How could she move on if they kept dragging her back to it?

'Where are you going?' Fin asked as she launched to her feet.

'To tell them if they don't move soon, they'll feel the wrath of one of your bra trebuchets.'

Fin's laugh was worth every nervous flutter as she strode up to the door and yanked it open. 'If you don't—*Mum!*'

'Darling, be a good girl and let us in, won't you? Your father's about to lamp one of these blighters, and I don't fancy seeing *that* in the headlines come morning.'

Her mother bustled past her, her father backing his way in behind, fists raised.

'Dad?!'

'Granny! Grandad!' Fin came racing up, arms outstretched, his grin true and wide. 'I'm so happy to see you!'

And so was she.

Tearful. Weary. But relieved.

Because as Matteo had taught her, a loving family was a blessing, a rock to lean on no matter the chaotic shape it took.

She only wished Matteo had the same.

Matteo waited for his father to flip the sign on his restaurant door to Closed before stepping from the shadows.

His father did a double take on the other side of the glass before turning away, and Matteo's stomach bottomed out. His father's message clear. So much for…

But then he was back, the door easing open. 'I'm so glad you've come. I've sent everyone away. Please…come in.'

So that's what he was doing, getting rid of an audience. Matteo supposed he should feel grateful, but he had no room for any more emotion. It was enough to force himself to walk forward and comply.

The restaurant was traditional and homely in every way. An abundance of dark wood, terracotta walls, fragrant flowers and small round tables that could be pushed together with ease. At the back was a bar, which his father stepped behind now.

'Drink?'

Matteo nodded, sinking into a seat at a table and willing his stomach to settle.

His father brought over a bottle and two glasses, sloshed a good measure of the clear spirit into each before sitting back. The ancient building creaked, outside the distant buzz of people and the sea rolled, but within, neither spoke, only stared.

For the first time in his life, Matteo took in the man that was his father. He'd seen photos over the years, known what he looked like, but never really *looked* at him.

And, *Dio*, it was like looking in the mirror thirty years down the line.

'I know,' his father said thickly. 'I can't get past it either. Lorenzo told me, but seeing it for myself, the resemblance is remarkable.'

Matteo winced as he took a swig of the grappa. 'Lorenzo has a lot to answer for.'

'It wasn't his fault. I begged him to tell me all he could.'

'You could have found out all you needed by coming to me yourself.'

'I know and I'm sorry. *Scusami tanto.*'

'Saying sorry doesn't change what you did. I want to know why. Why, in all the years that have gone by, you never tried to make contact. Not once!'

His father wet his lips, took an unsteady breath. 'You know our families separated us when we were young, young and without any autonomy over our lives... I tried to fight it, but it was no use. Back then, people lived in fear of my family, and your mother's, well, they feared them too, and they also feared for their reputation.'

'You're not telling me anything I don't already know.'

'No, but I need you to know that I fought. Fought like a man possessed for a long time. But your mother, she vanished, and I had no means of tracing her. At first, I didn't know where she'd gone, whether she was still in the country. There were rumours she'd gone to the UK, but they were just that—rumours. We didn't have social media, the internet was only small, it wasn't easy to track someone down. And then, by the time she was in the public eye, it was because of *you*. A rising star in the world of football...'

His eyes shone with pride, and Matteo quashed the feelings rising to greet it.

'So you knew I was your son?'

'Certamente.'

Matteo struck his fist against the table. 'Then, why not *then*? When you knew? Who I was and where she was? Why not *then*?'

'How could I? By then my family had fallen on hard times, been pushed out by the circles we moved in, and I was trying to make a life for my— for my family now. We didn't have much to our name. If I had come to you then with all your success and your wealth, I knew how the press would play it. How you and even your mother would see it after so many years.'

'At least you would have given us the opportunity to decide that for ourselves.'

'I had my family here to think of too. My wife and my three children.'

Matteo clenched his jaw against the pain, reached for his drink.

'I loved your mother. I was devastated to learn she'd passed away.'

Matteo choked on the grappa, its burn not enough

for the grief or the bitterness taking over. 'You don't know what love is.'

Because if it had been him and someone had taken Porsha away, he wouldn't have rested until he'd found her.

And woe betide the fools who had thought to take her from him.

'You are wrong. I loved Maria and she was taken from me.'

He scoffed, his father's words colliding with his thoughts.

'Loved her so much that you found someone else to take her place.'

'I fell in love again, yes. I will not deny that.'

Matteo shook his head, dismissing it even as his father laid his heart bare. The love lost and love gained written in every deep line of his face, his tortured gaze too.

'And there it is, the real reason you didn't come back to us. Your new love, your new family, they mattered more. We were replaced.'

'No, Matteo. Nothing could ever replace either of you. I mourned you. The two of you. But I accepted it was for the best. No one deserved the pain my return would have caused. To you, to your mother, to my wife and to my family here. The upheaval…'

'The upheaval would have settled and you could have been something to me. *Meant* something! Mum could have—'

'Could have what? Known me with my wife now?

My family? I know she never remarried. I know she was not as—' his throat bobbed '—fortunate.'

Matteo finished his drink and poured another, ignoring the sting behind his eyes. He would *not* cry for this man.

'The press would have ripped us apart. It was too late for me to play the proud father, and you were happy. Your mother was happy.'

'She never stopped loving you,' he said between his teeth, desperate not to feel any more.

'And I her. I did, I swear it. I still love Maria in here.' He pressed an unsteady hand to his chest.

'You left her with a pedestal so high she could never find happiness in another man.'

'And it is my deepest regret. That and all the years I missed out on being a father to you. Please, I don't expect you to forget the past, but I would like the opportunity to get to know you now. The opportunity to earn your forgiveness too.'

Matteo gave an abrupt nod. It wasn't an agreement, but neither was it a refusal. It would take time. He also realised that though he resembled his father, he was more like his mother inside. Because he too, had that pedestal, and Porsha was on it. The only woman for him and he'd pushed her away.

But unlike his parents, he was the only force at work keeping them apart.

How wrong he'd been.

Because there was no doubt in his mind that his heart belonged to Porsha and always would. The question was, would she accept it?

CHAPTER EIGHTEEN

Two days later

MATTEO RANG THE bell and stood back.

His neck prickled, telling him he wasn't alone. That somewhere in the street, hiding behind the many cars, trees and windows, reporters hovered, waiting for an update on their scoop, but he was done hiding. From himself at any rate.

And though he hated provoking the attention his notoriety had already brought Porsha's way, he couldn't bear waiting a second more. Couldn't bear the idea of sending a car or a message or someone else to do what he had to.

Footsteps sounded down the hall, a colourful silhouette visible through the frosted glass. The locks clicked, one after the other—how many locks?

Finally, the door creaked open, but the dark-haired woman before him wasn't Porsha. She was at least twenty years older and a riot of colour. From the band tied around her braided hair to the flowing dress that reached the floor.

'Can I help you? Oh!' Her green eyes widened as she placed a hand to her chest. 'You're him!'

'Mum, who is it?'

He stepped forward at the sound of Porsha's voice, needing more, craving more—and the door promptly closed in his face.

The voices built within and he rocked on his toes.

Please, Porsha. Please.

'*Cazzo*!' Not caring about his hidden audience, he ducked to the letterbox and pushed it open. 'Porsha, please, I just need to talk to you!'

He'd stooped to a new low, but if it meant she gave him the chance to speak...

Someone else came forward, a fuzzy blob of pink behind the glass... *Porsha?*

He straightened as the door eased open, and big hazel eyes—eyes that had haunted his every waking moment—blinked up at him. Dazed and amazed.

'*Please*, can I come in?'

She looked past him to the street, searching for the reporters, he was sure, and nodded, stepping aside just enough to let him in before promptly closing the door again.

'That's your...?' He gestured ahead to where the other woman was disappearing into the family room.

'Yes. Mum and Dad are here to help with Fin,' she said, heading up the stairs, and he followed her without question, guessing Fin was in the family room, and she wanted to put as much distance between him and their conversation as possible. 'They're going to take him after school for me too.'

'You asked them?'

'They came when they saw my face splashed across the papers.'

He bit back a curse.

'But I asked them to stay.'

His heart eased a fraction. At least something good had come from the mess he had made. To know that Porsha had opened up her life, Fin's life, to let her parents back in. To realise that the boy needed them just as much as she did.

'That's good.'

She said nothing.

Upstairs, boxes lined the hall. The floors were bare, and the walls were stripped, many a crack crying out for filler. But the only cracks he cared about were the ones he'd created between himself and the woman before him.

She pushed open the door to what must be her makeshift study. More boxes, bare floors, stripped walls and a contemporary white desk with a laptop set up before the window and a token plant flourishing in the late-afternoon sun.

'Excuse the mess,' she said, closing the door once he was inside and he had a flashback to that very first day they'd met... The same words spoken but *oh*, how they felt like different people. The world felt different.

'This has nothing on me right now.' He raked an unsteady hand through his hair. Well aware that he looked as haggard as he felt. 'I'm sorry, Porsha. I'm sorry I abandoned you in Capri. I'm sorry I didn't say goodbye to Fin. I'm sorry that the press caught wind and are all over you both. Harassing you. Writing crap about you...'

She was shaking her head, her bottom lip quivering and breaking his heart in two. 'Please stop. You don't need to apologise. I get that you feel bad about the press attention, but I brought it on myself, I brought it on us, Matteo. I knew what I was getting into with you. It isn't your fault.'

'Like hell it isn't.' He stepped towards her and she shrank back. 'I'm sorry. I'm not doing a very good job of explaining myself.'

'No, it's me who's sorry...' She wrapped her arms around her middle, the fluffy pink jumper such an unusual choice for her that Matteo's brow furrowed, and she read his thoughts as if he had said them aloud.

'It's my mum's,' she said, her smile meek. 'She declared my wardrobe *unsuitable breakup material.*'

'It suits you.'

Her nose wrinkled.

'Not the breakup,' he hurried out, 'but the colour! You know I *love* you in colour.'

Her eyes shone in the amber light streaking through the window, her glossy lips parted...*love*. He'd used the word *love* and it had been as loaded as his heart felt. Fit to burst from his chest at any moment.

He held her gaze as the air around them grew heavy. Longing caught up in all the hurt.

'You have no need to be sorry,' he whispered. 'What you did, you did because you cared.'

She shook her head.

'No?'

'Yes, I *cared*. But it was thoughtless and cruel. I should have spoken to you first, convinced you to go see him on your own, not walked you there myself, blindsiding you. I was too convinced it would work, that the moment you saw one another, you would realise how much he cared, and I got carried away by the opportunity, by us being there on the island where he lived...' She lowered her gaze and gripped her middle tighter. 'It was the wrong time to be impulsive. I should have weighed up the risks and realised it was wrong.'

'*No*.' He stepped forward, unable to stop himself, took hold of her fluffy-pink arms. 'You could have talked to me all you liked, and I doubt I would have changed my mind. It took that moment to snap me out of it, to break through the ice and realise you were right.'

'I was right?' Her lashes lifted, her eyes damp and unsure.

'Yes. Though it took a rant with my therapist to truly see it. And even then, there was more to understand.'

'More?'

'I took my anger and my pain out on you.'

'I know. But you had every right to be angry and hurt, after what happened with your father…'

'That's just it, the anger and the pain of old had nothing on the anger and pain I felt over you.'

Porsha blinked up at him, her gut rolling like the sea in a storm. His words sticking the knife in. 'I told you I was sorry. I really—'

'But you don't need to be sorry. Don't you see? It was all my own doing.'

'I don't understand.'

'Neither did I until Isabella walked me through it.'

'Care to walk me through it too, because…' Because inside she didn't know whether she was coming or going. Whether this was a continuation of the end or the start of something new.

'I lost sight of my greatest fear in my anger.'

'Your fear of being abandoned?'

Because of course she knew that's where his heart was at, anyone outside looking in would know it, and it's why her heart ached for him. Why her love for him had grown even as she'd forced herself to accept it could never be.

'But my father's presence should have allayed

my fear of that, it should have been the sign I needed that he wanted to know me. Instead that fear grew exponentially. Because in that moment, I was faced with the man who had broken my mother's heart…and the woman who had stolen mine so completely. The woman whose loss would far outweigh any other pain.'

'I don't understand,' she repeated numbly, because he couldn't mean…he couldn't be saying…

'I swore I'd never fall in love, Porsha. I swore I'd never give someone else the power to hurt me on that scale. And yet, you took it.'

'I took it?'

'The power…and my heart.'

She was shaking her head, her pulse was racing, her eyes were blurring with unshed tears. 'But you told me to go, you told me…'

'I know. I know. And I can't bear it. I can only say that I was scared, that rather than acknowledge my true feelings for you, I pushed them away. I pushed you away. Lashing out and doing what I feared most—losing you.'

'But you *love* me?'

He nodded, gave her a smile that was so forlorn she choked on her own tears.

'I do. And I had to come here and tell you. I'm done being scared, Porsha, and if you'll give me a second chance, I'll prove it to you. I promise I'll prove it to you.'

She pressed her fingers to her lips and let the

tears fall. Let his words sink in, let them warm her heart and fill her soul.

'You know, for a man who's run from love his entire life, you're quite poetic about it now. Is this Isabella talking or...'

He gave a choked chuckle. 'This is all me, I'm afraid.'

'Good.' She lifted her arms around his neck, pulled him closer and told him with her eyes as well as her words. 'Because I love you too.'

'You do?'

She nodded. 'I love you with all of my heart.'

He swept the hair from her face, his eyes glistening as they blazed down into hers. 'I'll never tire of hearing those words from your lips, *amore mio*.'

My love. She didn't need Google for that one.

'Good, because I plan on saying them every day from here on out. I'm not going anywhere, now or ever, though we better go downstairs soon because there's a boy who's desperate to see you.'

'And I him.'

'But first...'

She kissed him. Kissed him with all the love and hope for the future she never thought possible.

And everything she could ever want for him, for Fin, for them. A family.

EPILOGUE

Buckinghamshire, South East England
Two years later

'I THINK THE football pitch might have been a bit OTT,' Porsha said, leaning back against Matteo as they surveyed the land that was now their home.

Two years in the making, it was a blend of Georgian splendour and contemporary glamour, or so Porsha had informed him.

Location had been Matteo's priority. On the commuter belt for London but encased in countryside. Fresh air and green fields for as far as the eye could see, but close enough to civilisation for her to work, Fin to see his friends and Matteo... well, Matteo was happy because he had everything he wanted right here.

'Not the indoor pool?' he murmured, nibbling at her ear as she hugged his arms across her front, her engagement ring catching the light of the setting sun. 'When he has all his friends over from the De Luca youth centre, you'll be glad for that pitch, I promise you.'

She turned into him, her voice low and sultry. 'And you know what I think of your promises…'

'You know what I think of you repaying your debts too…'

She shivered, her eyes sparkling, the memories rising and charging the air around them.

'Do you think we can…?'

'With your mother and father about to arrive for the weekend?'

'They'll only love you all the more for it…though Fin less so, he's witnessed enough of the *lovey-dovey* stuff.'

He chuckled. 'He's going to have to get used to it with the wedding next week.'

'I imagine he'll be more distracted by his super-important role as best man—it was sweet of you to ask him.'

'I couldn't think of anyone else I'd rather have. He and Rodrigo make the perfect duo.'

'True.' She stroked her hands over his shoulders, curving her body into his. 'And how do you feel about your bride being one too?'

He frowned down at her. 'A duo?'

She nodded.

'Ha, I only need one bride, thank you very— wait!' There was something about the way her brows had lifted, her eyes had welled up…

'Porsha, are you…are we…?'

'I'm pregnant, Matteo.'

He opened his mouth to speak but nothing came out, tears filling his eyes as his heart soared.

'I think Fin's going to make an amazing big brother, don't you?' she said.

He nodded, still too choked to speak.

'And you *are* happy? Because you're looking a bit…shellshocked.'

'I don't know what to say, Porsha. When you and Fin came into my life, you gave me everything I'd never known I was missing. To be a dad, I never thought, I never imagined…'

She cupped his cheeks. 'You may not have thought it or imagined it, but I tell you now, you will be the best father to our child, and you know how I know this?'

He shook his head within her hands. 'Because you have been the *best* father to Fin. And you will be the *best* husband to me. And together we will make the happiest Lucky Luca-Lang family the world has ever seen!'

'Lucky Luca-Lang?!'

She stole his chuckle with her kiss and he felt her words in his very bones.

This was family.

Everything he could ever need or want.

And even if it was an addiction of sorts, it was one he could wholly get on board with and dedicate his life to.

Because this was love.

* * * * *